DARBY AND JOAN

by

Maurice Baring

Dales Large Print Books
Long Preston, North Yorkshire,
BD23 4ND, England.

British Library Cataloguing in Publication Data.

Baring, Maurice
    Darby and Joan.

    A catalogue record of this book is
    available from the British Library

    ISBN   978-1-84262-567-5 pbk

First published in Great Britain in 1935

Copyright © The Trustees of the Maurice Baring Will Trust

Cover illustration © Ben Turner by arrangement with
P.W.A. International Ltd.

The right of Maurice Baring to be identified as the author of
this work has been asserted

Published in Large Print 2008 by arrangement with
A P Watt Literary, Film & Television Agents

Dales Large Print is an imprint of Library Magna Books Ltd.

Printed and bound in Great Britain by
T.J. (International) Ltd., Cornwall, PL28 8RW

Dedicated
To
Conrad Russell

NOTE

This story is true. It happened between 1546 and 1629. I have transposed the dates to 1855 and 1930. I have not had to invent *what* happened, but only to try and guess *how* it happened. What I have said happened, happened. I have been obliged to foreshorten the time spaces and thereby to dilute the spirits of truth, which, undiluted, are too raw for the drinker of fiction. For in fiction there is a degree of truth which is *trop vrai pour être toléré*.

My thanks are due to Mr Edward Marsh for correcting the proofs.

CHAPTER 1

Joan Brendon was the second daughter of Robert, the only son of Sir James Payne Brendon, Bart., a country gentleman.

James Brendon had married a penniless beauty and thus incurred the anger of his father, who had left everything except his house to a younger brother. James Brendon's wife died young, leaving him one daughter besides Robert; he himself was killed out hunting, and Robert was left with a house in Suffolk he could neither sell nor afford to keep up. He let it.

Robert spent the years of his youth attached to embassies and legations in different European cities – Paris, Berlin, Florence, Lisbon. In 1850, when he was thirty, he married a daughter of a Lord Swynford, whose brother was British Minister at Florence, and whose wife was an Italian. Robert left the Service as soon as he was married, owing to ill-health. He had been a sufferer from asthma from his school days, and he had inherited a tendency to gout from his father. Robert and his wife lived abroad, not only for his health's sake but for economy – they were poor. At first they wintered at

Nice: then they settled down in Florence for good, and bought a little villa on the Fiesole side of the river. Mrs Brendon was delicate; she barely survived the birth of a daughter who died soon after she was born in 1852, and she herself died giving birth to Joan in 1855.

Robert did not come back to England. He had few friends there, and he found the society that suited him in the South of France or in Florence. He was a quiet, un-ambitious, cultivated man, with a square face and whiskers, saturated in the traditions of the eighteenth century, whose writers in French and in English he was devoted to. As a young man he had been fond of riding and sport, but asthma and gout soon made these impossible, and he devoted himself to quieter hobbies, such as painting – he painted deli-cately finished watercolours which faithfully represented the hills and silvery olive trees he was fond of – and botany when he felt strong enough. The lodestar of his life was his daughter, Joan.

Joan was baptized a Catholic and brought up first by a nurse, Kathleen O'Keefe, who came from Ireland, and was steeped in Irish traditions, and later by a German governess, Fräulein Krauss, known as Tishy, who had a genius for teaching, and taught Joan not only German but to speak French with neither an English nor a German accent. She gave her a good grounding in common sense, and instilled into her the German love of household ritual, birthday cakes, Christmas trees, picture-books, garlands and nosegays. She tried to teach her music but failed, for Joan was tone-deaf. She had begun to teach her history and geography, but Tishy died when Joan was ten, and Joan's further education was conducted by her father, who, although lazy, gout-ridden, and totally without any understanding of children, could not bear the thought of getting another governess. Thus it was that Joan's scholastic education stopped short at the cultivated court not of the Empress Josephine but of William the Conqueror. The rest of the history of the world she had to pick up as best she could by herself.

Joan was a shy and rather awkward child, and given to fits of passionate naughtiness, but her father soon found out she was the most intelligent of companions. He found he could talk to her as if she were a grown-up person, and he did. Robert Brendon was a strange mixture. The outside world thought him cynical, and indeed his mind and his conversation would often reveal a vein of sharp and polished irony; but there was also in his composition a layer of rigid principle as hard as a rock. A breach of manners, a spiritual or intellectual solecism, and still more any act or word that betrayed a want of tact or a lapse in taste, or a suspicion of conduct that infringed his fastidious code of what was befitting and what was impossible, affected him as a wrong note affects a musician, and made him inwardly wince or shiver, although he would make no comment, and only betray his disapproval by a certain sudden deadly silence.

Robert Brendon dreaded having to undertake Joan's education, but when he came to do it he found it quite easy. That is to say, he found himself completely at his ease with her. It is true he taught her on a system which was entirely his own, and was really no system at all. He taught her what he was interested in himself at the time: French memoirs, Musset's verse, Racine, Lamartine, chemical experiments, to enjoy Old Masters, perspective, a little astronomy; Pope, Dryden, but not Shakespeare, who bored him; he instilled into her his early enthusiasm for Lord Byron and his lasting love of botany. He took her to picture galleries and churches; he took her to Rome and Naples and Paestum. Although, owing to her nurse's insistence, she was baptized by a Catholic priest, Joan was taught no religion at all except what she gathered from Tishy and from her nanny. Her father disliked parsons and had a horror of what he called 'quarter-to-eleven church'. On the other hand, he looked upon Catholicism as an interesting historical institution founded on dogmas in which no reasonable person could believe, but offering a sensible code of morals, and overlaid with a mass of superstitions which, although possibly regrettable, were picturesque, a boon to art, and not more silly, and less changeable, than the superstitions of men of science. On the other hand, he had no anti-religious prejudices; he was a complete agnostic and enjoyed a position of speculative doubt; he was interested in all creeds just as he was interested in all quaint customs; but he thought that as religion often led to trouble and unpleasantness it was best to meddle with it as little as possible. Joan should believe whatever she liked, and he felt it reassuring that Kathleen's fervent superstition was counteracted by Tishy's solid and downright Lutheranism. Neither the one nor the other had much effect on Joan, who, when she was eight years old, confronted her father with the mystery of evil, a problem which he said he was unable to solve, although he assured her it had given many others considerable food for thought. 'Both theologians and philosophers,' he said, 'have always found it puzzling.'

Nanny said that such questions were prompted by the devil. Tishy merely said: 'Ach was! Du bist zu neugierig.'

So Joan made up her mind that grown-up people never would talk sensibly when you

17

wanted them to, and created a religion of her own. She made her tortoise, 'Childe Harold', into a minor household deity, and she prayed to him if it thundered – she was afraid of thunder – but if she lost her handkerchief or anything else she invoked St Anthony of Padua, a proceeding which she found was surprisingly successful, and if she wanted anything she asked Santa Claus. Kathleen tried to make her say her rosary, but Joan said it made her giddy. As she grew older and read books – and her father let her read everything – her early doubts were confirmed, and by the time she was seventeen she was just as much of an agnostic as her father. But he taught her to respect shrines and holy places because, he said, 'one never knows. It may be true.' He even encouraged her to put up candles to the saints. 'Why not be on the safe side?' he used to say. 'We must always remember that men of science are just as bigoted as churchmen, and know just as little.' He was fond, too, of saying that when disbelief was made into a creed it was less reasonable than any religion.

Apart from her father, Joan had few companions. The children of Robert's Italian friends and of the other English residents in Florence bored her. Once or twice she made friends with some English boys at Nice, and when she was fifteen she had a short boy-and-girl flirtation with a gay American. She preferred boys to girls, and grown-up people to both, and to all grown-up people her father, whom she worshipped.

Until Joan was seventeen she was looked upon as an ugly duckling, a sallow, rather untidy, awkward creature, with rebellious dark hair and inky hands – she was always painting or making something, or dabbling in chemicals, or digging up plants. She had a small aquarium and a rock-garden. She had, if a lonely, an enjoyable childhood, the only serious cloud being the death of Tishy. It was not until Joan was over seventeen that her father realized she was grown up; she was indeed, although utterly ignorant and un-educated in some ways, extremely advanced and precocious in others. It was one October morning, when she and her father were looking at the pictures in the Pitti Gallery, that two French tourists passed them, elegant, and people of the world – the man dressed with care, the woman with the simplicity that means the last word of fashion and expense. They were, Brendon thought, husband and wife; they were volubly discussing the pictures, and the man was making suggestive and witty comments. The man was about thirty; he had a beard and wore an eyeglass with a tortoiseshell rim on a large black ribbon. As he passed Joan and her father he gave Joan one quick look of sudden and final appraisement and certain appreciation, and after he had passed on he made some comment to his wife which evidently referred to Joan, for the lady, as soon as she could do so without incivility, managed to glance at Joan. Brendon was aware that his daughter had been admired by a man of the world and a man of taste. This gave him a shock. He realized that Joan's childhood was over, and that she must come out. That very afternoon he called on his sister-in-law, who was his sole real friend in Florence and whom he visited constantly: this was Countess Mabel San Felice, his wife's sister, and now a widow with grown-up daughters of her own. She had never had looks, but she had something perhaps even better, a face that made everyone wish they were like her; an expression of transparent sincerity, eyes that were wells of good-natured fun.

Robert found her at home in her villa at Bellosguardo, by herself. After the Countess had given him tea and they had talked a little on the topics of the day:

'You haven't brought Joan. The children are out, but they will be back soon.'

'I haven't brought her because I want to talk about her. She will be eighteen next April.'

'Have you only just found that out, *caro?* I've known it for a long time.'

'Don't laugh at me. I only found it out this

morning. I'm so used to her being a child, but this morning we went to the Pitti, and a Frenchman and his wife – he good-looking and she well-dressed–'

'That's Monsieur and Madame de Neufchateau,' said Mabel. 'They called here yesterday.'

'Well, they passed us and he looked at Joan.'

'He would. He is a connoisseur.'

'And I think he admired her.'

'Don't you?'

'I always thought Joan was the ugly duckling.'

'Yes, but you know what happens to ugly ducklings – they grow into swans.'

'You don't think Joan is pretty?'

'Pretty is not the word. She's more than that.'

'She'll never be what's called handsome, she's too small and too short.'

'You forget that children at that age are unformed. They are like puppies. Joan has got a neat figure, what will be a very good figure, and you will find that people will always like looking at her.'

'Her nanny says that if she hadn't always lived abroad and if she had some colour, she would be a beauty.'

'That pale skin of hers is attractive with those eyes.'

'Yes, she has got eyes, and I suppose she

will be attractive,' said Robert, with a sigh. 'That will make it all the worse. However, I always tell her to remember that she hasn't got a classic nose, only the makings of a classic nose; it started classic and finished baroque.'

'She's going to be very attractive indeed, and more than that. She has quality – something genuine and noble – like a piece of good silver, or a Stradivarius, or a real Old Master, and as she gets older that will become more and more marked.'

Robert sighed again.

'I believe you are right; all that makes it all the more difficult for me. I don't know what to do with her. When she sees people she never says a word, but she says most surprising things to me – most surprising – and she is always asking me questions I can't answer; and then she is a bad needle-woman.'

The Countess laughed.

'Do you think that is essential?'

'Perhaps not essential, but Joan takes no interest in needlework at all. With strangers she is silent.'

'That's shyness, and as it should be, now.'

'Well,' said Robert, 'the fact of the matter is, I suppose, the time has come when she ought to go out. I ought to take her to London, and how can I do it? I can't go to balls, I can hardly walk about the house.'

It was true that Robert's gout, and more serious still his asthma, grew worse every year.

'The truth of it is, my dear friend,' he said after a pause, 'I'm finished, and I know it. I am not only an invalid and a cripple, but I am like an old broken pair of bellows and fit for the dust-heap.'

'Oh, nonsense, Robert, don't talk like that. I will take Joan out this winter here, for what there is to offer, and in the spring couldn't she go to London and stay with some of her relations?'

'Well, who is there? There is only her Aunt Emily, or my sister Amy who married Horace Cantillon, and that's about all.'

'But wouldn't that do? Haven't they got a daughter?'

'Yes, one – Agatha. She's just out.'

'Well, that's the very thing.'

'Horace and Amy would be kind to her – but she wouldn't go – she wouldn't leave me.'

'Could you take a house in London and let her aunt take her out?'

'Yes, we might do that in the summer – I couldn't live through an English winter. She'll be eighteen in April,' he said.

'Well, it won't be in the least too late. I am against girls coming out too soon.'

'And it means we must find her a husband.'

'Of course.'

'I could trust you to find her one, my dear friend, but no one else. It will be difficult to find someone worthy of her. Very.'

'It always is.'

'I think the young men of the present day insupportable.'

'Oh! they always were.'

'I suppose so. We were certainly insufferable. And then she'll probably fall in love with some impossible fellow.'

'I don't think Joan will.'

'One never knows. I wish we had *mariages de convenance* in England. They are so much more sensible. But with Joan it would be out of the question. You see, she takes after her dear mother, and her dear mother insisted on marrying me against all advice and all the canons of common sense. Joan will do what she pleases. She knows what she likes and says so. She gets that from her mother.'

'Some of the Careggis *are* clever,' said the Countess. 'Some not at all. Joan is *very* clever.'

'Yes, clever is a stupid word, but she is it. She knows nothing, and she knows too much. That's my fault. Her real education stopped when Fräulein died, and I have done nothing but miseducate her, and not teach her what she should know.'

'Joan will always know quite enough.'

'Well, she is sensible; I can say that for her.

Then there's another question, a question of great importance,' said Robert. 'She's got no clothes. She must have something to wear.'

'Leave that to me,' said the Countess.

And at that moment their conversation was interrupted by the arrival of her two grown-up girls, who were loud in their regrets at not seeing Joan. Robert took his leave and drove home in the shut carriage to his villa.

Robert's villa was on the hillside. On one side of it, looking west, there was a small loggia opening out on a terrace with a low balustrade, and two short flights of steps leading to the garden, a paved garden with flowers in pots and tubs. Robert got out at the gate of the villa, which was on the south-side, and sent the carriage on, but instead of walking round to the front door, which was on the opposite side to the loggia, he walked towards the steps and saw Joan standing against the balustrade of the terrace. She was looking at the sunset. There had been a brief thunderstorm earlier in the afternoon. The sky had now been washed clean and was splashed with watery gold in the west, but high up in the east there were still some soft billowy grey clouds, sharp in outline, like the countries of a fantastic continent, and suffused with a pink glow. There was a glory as of silent music in the air. Joan was watching the sunset absorbed. She was dressed in white, with a shawl hanging down from one shoulder, like a piece of drapery. She did not look too small in that setting. She was as well proportioned as a Tanagra. Robert thought of Iphigenia; 'Ready,' he said to himself with a sigh, 'for the sacrifice.' She did not notice her father – she was looking at the sky.

After watching her for a moment, her father walked up the drive to the front door and went through the house into the loggia and out to the terrace. Joan was still there. He went up to her on tiptoe. She did not notice him till he was quite close to her and called her.

'Oh! how you startled me, Papa,' she said, and her eyes lit up with pleasure.

'Yes,' thought Robert, 'she is grown up.'

CHAPTER 2

Robert Brendon was exhausted by his visit and by the short walk from the garden to the house, but in spite of his fatigue he wrote to his sister Amy and told her he had decided to bring Joan to London, as it was high time she came out. He talked about taking a house, and he asked her to help him. He was in a hurry now to get the matter settled. He felt he had already put it off too long. He felt guilty towards Joan; but, more than anything, he felt he had not got much longer to live.

He broached the subject at dinner that night to Joan.

'I am going to take you to London, this summer,' he said. 'It will be good for both of us.'

Joan looked at him and smiled.

'That will be fun,' she said, as cheerfully as she could, but her heart sank. She knew it would be impossible for her father to travel, and she divined that he must be feeling really ill to think of such a thing. In fact she followed what actually had been the process of his mind.

'I have written to your Aunt Amy and

asked her to find us a little house. She's clever about that kind of thing. I haven't been to London for twenty years.'

Joan smiled. She felt there was nothing to say.

'I talked to your Aunt Mabel about it, and she agreed it was a capital idea Do you think you will like it?'

'I shall be happy anywhere as long as I am with you, Papa. You know that – don't you?'

'Yes, I do.' His eyes filled with tears. 'I've been selfish all my life and culpable towards you, but...' He couldn't go on, and he gasped for breath.

'Oh, don't, Papa! Nobody has ever had a happier childhood than I have. You are never to say such a thing again.'

They talked of other things, and after dinner Joan read to him aloud a novel by Georges Sand.

A few days later Countess San Felice came to luncheon with them. Joan took her to the garden after luncheon, and her aunt talked to her of the future and of London.

'Your father has set his heart,' she said, 'on taking you to London.'

'Yes, I know, Aunt Mabel,' said Joan, 'but I don't think London would be good for him.'

'But couldn't you perhaps stay with your Aunt Amy?'

'And leave Papa alone here?'

Joan seemed to grow whiter than usual.

'I couldn't do that. I could never leave Papa alone,' she said, and the Countess knew this was final.

'The change might do him good in the summer,' said the Countess. 'He would like to be there when you come out and see you enjoy yourself.'

'I enjoy myself much more with him than with anyone else,' said Joan. 'I do not want to go to London; I daren't tell Papa that because it would disappoint him; but I know we shall never go to London together.'

The Countess felt Joan was right, but she said:

'I think he is looking much better.'

'He has dreadful nights,' said Joan, 'and he won't have a nurse.'

'It is a pity, and it's wrong, and it's wearing you out – you look so tired, *poverina*.'

'I'm never tired; I like looking after him. You see there is so little time left,' and she looked at her aunt quietly, and in her eyes, which were sometimes grey and sometimes blue, there was an immense sadness.

Her aunt could not contradict her.

'That is why you must never think me rude or ungracious, Aunt Mabel,' Joan continued, 'when I refuse your invitations. I come when he can come; when he is up to it. It amuses him and he loves it and it's good for him, but when he can't, then I stay with him. I want to be with him every minute I can.'

'Well, *cara,*' said the Countess, 'you know how fond I am of him and of you, and that I am always here when you want me.'

Robert called to them from the loggia, and that was all they said on the matter; but from that moment they understood each other perfectly. The Countess felt that Joan was exaggerating nothing, and she wondered whether Robert would live through the winter.

A few days later Robert Brendon received a letter from his sister Amy suggesting that he and Joan should come and stay with her in the summer. When he told Joan of this she agreed that it might be pleasant. But nothing was arranged and everything went on as before, except that Countess San Felice still invited Joan to her house whenever she had guests, and Joan went there when her father felt up to it, and whenever she thought it would amuse him. Joan's views of her father's condition were not exaggerated. His asthma was worse than it had ever been. He got little sleep, and his gout was chronically bad. He was wheeled about in a chair and spent most of his time in the loggia of the villa. Nevertheless, whenever he heard of any English or foreign acquaintances coming to Florence, he was anxious to see them and invited them to luncheon. Joan often found herself a hostess. This was a revolution in

Robert Brendon's life, for up to now he had shrunk from the visits of guests and shunned English invaders like the plague.

Joan knew this was done for her, and tried all she could to prevent it, but she failed, and she knew it was better now to let him have his way than to oppose him.

It was a mild winter. After Christmas Robert's health began to improve, and by Easter he seemed to be better than he had been for a long time. It had been settled that he was to take Joan to London after Easter. They were to stay with his sister at first and look about for a house. They would stop in Paris on the way. Joan acquiesced in all these plans, but she doubted whether they would be realized.

It was during Easter week that Countess San Felice asked them to luncheon to meet some friends who were staying at Florence. They turned out to be Theodore Walton, a famous painter, and his young wife; and Monsieur and Madame de Neufchateau, the same couple whom Joan and her father had seen at the Pitti in October; a young man in the Brigade of Guards called Alexander Luttrell, whose father, Lord Carhampton, had been a friend of Robert's. Besides the guests, there was Countess San Felice's brother-in-law, Pietro San Felice, a handsome man of fifty, a traveller and a linguist, who had translated Lermontov's poems into Italian and

31

written a book on the English Masque. He acted as host.

It was just such an entertainment as Joan dreaded and disliked above all things. They were just the kind of guests who paralysed her with shyness: all of them talkative and cultivated; Walton ornate and eloquent, with a beard and large black tie tied in a bow, speaking French and Italian beautifully; Monsieur de Neufchateau saying exactly the right things about art and life, and now and then feeling obliged to counteract the extreme silliness of his wife's remarks, her intelligence being confined to her clothes (in that domain she was an artist of the first rank, and she made Joan feel as much ashamed of herself physically as the men made her feel ashamed of herself intellectually); Pietro San Felice, who, between rather complicated paradoxes, paid elaborate compliments; Rezia San Felice, the daughter of the house, who put her to shame by her ease. These were the elements with which she was confronted in the low cool living-room of the Villa San Felice. Her heart sank as she was introduced to the guests, but she knew her father would enjoy himself as much as she would dislike it. Then, to her surprise and delight, she saw one friendly face, that is to say, one face which had showed to her that here was someone she could be comfortable with among so much civility. It was Alexander Luttrell. There was a look of fun in his eyes, and she liked his whole appearance; he was thin, rather good-looking, without being showy; and she guessed by his expression, which had a lurking mockery in it, that he was unaffectedly amused at finding himself in such company; but what she liked best about him was the feeling that he was what Countess San Felice had said about her – genuine, not imitation.

Countess San Felice welcomed everyone enthusiastically, lamented the absence of her elder daughter, who was laid up with a cold, congratulated Robert on looking so well, and accepted with a radiant smile Monsieur de Neufchateau's compliments on herself, her daughter and her home. She then led the guests into the dining-room, where they sat at a round table.

Joan to her great joy found herself next to Alexander Luttrell, who at once said to her:

'Thank heavens we can talk English – I can't speak any foreign language.'

'Your other neighbour is English too,' Joan said to him in an undertone.

This was true. Madame de Neufchateau was an Englishwoman by birth, but she had lived in France a great deal, and although she could speak English perfectly she preferred to speak broken English with a slight French accent whenever she remembered to.

The conversation was more or less general.

The Neufchateaus were on their way back to Paris from Rome, where they had spent the winter.

Monsieur de Neufchateau said that Rome was no longer what it had been and complained of the number of his compatriots. Robert Brendon reminded him that Montaigne had made the same complaint.

He felt certain, he said, that foreign visitors after the expulsion of the kings had said that same thing: Rome was no longer what it was in Tarquin's day. San Felice explained that Rome in the days of the kings, far from being a pastoral hamlet, was a large industrial centre like Birmingham or Manchester. Walton became lyrical on the subject of the Campagna; Countess San Felice vehement on the vandalism of those in authority; Robert Brendon talked botany quietly with Mrs Walton, and Madame de Neufchateau said that St Peter's was disappointing.

'That's what it is, *disappointing*,' she repeated, triumphantly, as if she had by a miracle lighted upon a rare and exquisitely felicitous *mot juste*.

Joan felt entirely comfortable with Alexander Luttrell after they had exchanged two sentences. He was relieved to find she knew nothing about Florentine history.

Just as they were enjoying themselves in discussing their common ignorances, Walton turned to Joan and asked her whether she had ever been painted.

'Oh no,' she said, feeling absurdly awkward and shy.

'Well, when you come to London,' he said, 'you must let me paint you. I seldom meet people I want to paint, I promise you I have met one today – but perhaps you don't like my way of painting...?'

'I haven't ever seen any of your pictures,' said Joan. 'I have never been to England.'

'Well, you shall come to my studio when you are in London. Your father tells me you are coming this summer, and if you approve I will paint you.'

His attention was taken by the Countess, and presently Alexander Luttrell asked Joan whether Walton wanted to paint her.

'Yes,' she said, 'he says so.'

'He wouldn't say it if he didn't mean it.'

'Would he know how to?' she asked.

Alexander laughed. 'He is supposed to be one of the best living English painters.'

'Does that mean very much?'

Alexander laughed again:

'I'm not sure it does,' he said.

'Do you like his pictures?'

'I like his portraits, not his fantastic pictures. I think he would paint you very well.'

There was a note of admiration in his voice as he said this, and it was the first time Joan had ever heard this note. It was an extraordinary sensation to her. It made her swallow in a quick gulp the bit of food she was eating, and she felt she was turning scarlet; in reality it brought a faint touch of colour to her pale face, and it lit up her eyes. She looked at him and smiled. Alexander Luttrell looked at her, and he thought he had never seen such eyes in his life. Something stirred in him. He was aware that he felt something he had never felt before, but at that moment Madame de Neufchateau turned and asked him which he liked best, Florence or Rome?

Luttrell said Florence, but admitted he had not yet been to Rome.

'*Ce que je dis*,' she said, and then, changing to English, 'What I say is that Florence is Florence, but that *Rome* is *Rome*.'

Monsieur de Neufchateau, who was sitting opposite to his wife, screwed in his eyeglass and said good-humouredly:

'*C'est exact, ma chère.*'

Joan had no more opportunity of talking to Alexander Luttrell, for either his attention was monopolized by Madame de Neufchateau or hers by Walton, who talked to her eloquently about the cities of Italy and the countries of Europe – but, when the meal was over and coffee was served on the terrace, Robert Brendon talked to Luttrell and asked him to luncheon at his villa on the following Friday, and Luttrell accepted the invitation with alacrity.

CHAPTER 3

Alexander and Joan met again twice during the next week before the Friday, once at the Uffizi Gallery, where Joan and a certain Miss Van Lahmer who gave painting lessons, and used to teach Joan twice a week, were making copies of an Old Master. Miss Van Lahmer was deaf, absent-minded and absorbed in her work. Alexander asked for Joan's assistance as a guide, and they spent a little time looking at the pictures, comparing notes every now and then, but they ended by talking of other things. The time went so quickly by that Joan felt she had only been talking to Alexander for a few minutes when Miss Van Lahmer said it was time for them to go home for luncheon.

Before she left, Alexander Luttrell told her he had been invited to go for a drive and a picnic tea with the San Felices. Joan said she had been invited also, and was going.

'Then I will go too,' said Alexander.

The drive and picnic came off two days later. Joan and her father drove in their carriage, and they met at Alexander Luttrell's hotel, where they joined the San Felices' party, which consisted of the Countess, her two daughters, Angelica and Rezia, and two Italian boy cousins.

The Countess, Joan, her father and Alexander drove in one carriage and the young Italian folk in the other. They drove rather a long distance to a picturesque villa, belonging to friends of the Countess, uninhabited for the moment, which had a long grass terrace and a high wall and a rampart of cypresses, and there they had tea, and after tea the young people went for a walk, leaving Robert and the Countess at the villa. Joan and Alexander were thrown together, then separated, and then thrown together once more. They were never long alone together, but it so happened that, during the intervals of time in which they were together, a certain definite progress was established in their relations. A certain rubicon was crossed which could never be recrossed.

It was a hot April afternoon. The Florentine country was looking its loveliest. The Judas-trees were out, solid masses of blossom against the blinding blue. The hills were green with the growing corn: there were fringes of wild pink roses everywhere, right up to the corn, and Alexander said that people in England would think it odd if you talked of roses growing next to the wheat.

'That's because they've never seen the South,' said Joan. 'I suppose you can't guess what the South is like unless you've seen it.

I have never seen anything else. I have to guess what England's like. I have made up an England out of Tauchnitz novels, Miss Braddon, George Eliot, Anthony Trollope, Thackeray, Dickens, Ouida – I am longing to see it.' This led them to books.

Alexander was surprised at what she had read, not so much at the quantity as the quality – as she had mentioned naturally certain French novels that he knew no girl in England would be allowed to read.

'Papa lets me read anything,' she said, divining his thoughts. 'French and English. I have read *The Heart of Midlothian* and even *Peveril of the Peak*.'

'That's going too far,' said Alexander.

After Alexander and Joan had enjoyed a second interval of companionship and pauseless talk, the party came together again and got reshuffled, and Joan walked back to the villa with one of the young Italians. They then drove home.

The city of Florence appeared to them in the evening light like a fabric made of the same texture as flowers. Brunelleschi's Dome seemed ethereal; Giotto's Tower looked like a lily. When they reached the town they stopped. Goodbyes were said. The San Felices went their way. Robert dropped Alexander and went home with Joan. As he said goodbye Robert reminded him that he was to come to luncheon on Friday (the next day). Alexander looked at Joan as he said goodbye to her, and he thought – as the sun sank in glory in the west, and the shadows were dark on the Arno, with a few feathery clouds of rosy hue scattered high in the radiant vault of the east – that her grey eyes reflected the stillness of the evening.

He knew, and Joan knew, and each knew that the other knew, that something had happened to both of them. Neither of them would ever be again as if this had not been.

As they drove home Robert said to Joan:

'I like that young man – he's got good manners, and he's no fool.'

Joan said nothing.

Alexander came to luncheon at Villa Brendon the next day. Robert had asked no one else but Countess San Felice. He was not quite so well, and when luncheon was over he asked the Countess to follow him into his sitting-room as he had matters he wished to discuss with her, so Joan and Alexander were left together in the loggia.

Alexander said he was obliged to leave Florence on the following Sunday evening.

'But,' he said, 'we shall meet in London.'

'I wonder,' said Joan.

'But your father said he was starting in three weeks' time.'

'I hardly think he will be well enough to travel.'

'Well, if you don't come to London I shall

have to come back to Florence.'

Joan did not contradict him.

'But can't we meet before I leave?' he went on. 'My sister is arriving from Rome this evening, and I shall have to start back to London with her on Sunday whatever happens, because my leave is coming to an end.'

'You can come here,' said Joan. 'Papa will always be delighted to see you – he likes you.'

'Are you sure of that?'

'Quite sure; when he doesn't like someone he says nothing, but one knows it.'

'I will come tomorrow afternoon and pay him a formal visit. I want to ask him something.'

'They are coming,' said Joan, and at that moment Countess San Felice and Robert came into the room.

'Well,' said Robert to Joan, 'I hope you have been entertaining our guest, my dear.'

Alexander said he must go. The Countess offered him a lift in her carriage. She noticed that Joan's eyes were particularly bright.

'You must come again,' said Robert to Alexander.

'I'm sorry to say I've got to leave on Sunday, but I'll come tomorrow afternoon for a moment to say goodbye – if I may.'

'Yes do, yes do, if you have time,' said Robert absentmindedly. He was tired. Joan saw this at once.

'Papa, you must go and rest,' she said.

Goodbyes were said and the Countess took Alexander away with her. Joan took her father to his sitting-room, and settled him in an armchair. Presently he fell asleep.

He had not slept well the night before. Joan thought he looked ill. But other thoughts were racing through her brain. She was deliriously happy, and yet strangely frightened for the future.

When Alexander got back to the hotel he found a telegram from his sister telling him that instead of arriving at Florence that evening (Friday), she was arriving the next evening (Saturday), and asking him to meet her at the station. Alexander at once wrote and telegraphed to Joan that he would not be able to come to the villa at teatime the next day owing to his sister's change of plan, but that he would come on Sunday afternoon.

His sister arrived on Saturday afternoon as she said.

Lady Alice Haslewood was older than Alexander. She was fair, good-looking and gay, quick-witted, quick-tempered and sharp-tongued, rather fond of mischief, and she had married a rising politician older than herself who was a Member of Parliament.

She was full of plans and of energy. She wanted during her short stay at Florence to cram in all that was possible. Alexander said he was willing to do anything she liked, but that he was not free Sunday afternoon. He had to go to say goodbye to an old gentleman who had been kind to him.

Lady Alice wanted to know, who, why and what.

Alexander explained.

'I know,' said Lady Alice, 'there's a daughter, isn't there? What is she like?'

'Oh, very nice,' said Alexander dispassionately.

'Pretty?'

'Not exactly.'

Lady Alice understood that it was not to be civil to an old gentleman that Alexander was going to pay the visit.

'By the way,' said Lady Alice, 'Hilda and Charlie are here.'

She meant Colonel and Mrs Dasent: she was the wife of a soldier who had distinguished himself in the Crimea: she had been a great beauty, with light blue eyes and a dazzling complexion. She was still beautiful, but her want of distinction was now visible. Alexander had been at one time wildly in love with her, and she still regarded him as her property, although she had other admirers; but Alexander was the youngest. His infatuation had really been dead for some time, but nothing had happened until now to make him realize it. It happened now; Alexander was not pleased at the thought of seeing her.

'They're dining with us tonight,' said Lady Alice.

Alexander had to accept the situation. They all dined at a little café in the Via Tornabuom. At the table next to theirs, there was another party of English people whom they all knew. The picturesque and artistic Lady Tintagel, a patron of the arts and a lover of music, surrounded as usual by a bevy of attendants; among them was Basil D'Eynecourt, who sometimes wrote novels and sometimes composed songs – readable, but commonplace novels; tuneful, but not original songs. The two groups exchanged civilities and discussed and compared plans.

Mrs Dasent counted on Alexander spending the day with her, but he said he was lunching with some Italians, and had to pay a visit in the afternoon. He was not able to refuse her suggestion that he should take her to see the Pitti and the Boboli Gardens in the morning. This he did, and there again he met Lady Tintagel and her little court, and they once more exchanged civilities. In the meantime Joan Brendon had received Alexander's message with bitter disappointment, but she was looking forward to Sunday afternoon. Basil D'Eynecourt, who was anxious to escape at least for a meal from Lady Tintagel's suave but exacting tyranny, had proposed himself to luncheon with his old acquaintance, Robert Brendon, and Joan prayed he would not stay too long. They had no other guests. Joan remained silent at

luncheo   D'Eynecourt, who was
a beard   ss little man, retailed the
gossip   where he had been lately,
and of   he had just spent Easter.

'Last   aid, 'we saw Lady Alice
Haslev   r brother, Alexander, and
the Da   with them.'

'The   Robert asked. 'Oh, Charlie
Dasen   . Is he married?'

'Yes   sent and his wife, she was
a Miss   the daughter of a north
country manufacturer – very rich.'

'I don't think I ever saw her.'

'She *was* lovely. She made a sensation
when they were first married. She's still very
good-looking, although one sees *now* she's a
little bit common. Before, she was so lovely
that one didn't see that, or, if one did, one
didn't care. However, Alexander Luttrell
seems to find her just as lovely as ever.'

Joan felt she was turning to stone.

'Was he attracted by her?' Robert asked.

'Oh, he was very much in love with her, and
it's been going on for a long time. Some
people in London said it was all over, but it
evidently isn't. We met them again at the Pitti
this morning and he seemed just as adoring
as ever, only that means nothing where
Alexander is concerned. Like all his family,
he can never resist a pretty face, and I'm
afraid he's not only impressionable but fickle
– very fickle. She's an attractive woman, and

45

good-natured too. Charlie's as deaf as a post now.'

Basil D'Eynecourt went rattling on, but Joan couldn't listen to what he was saying.

D'Eynecourt left as soon as they had drunk coffee, and Robert said to Joan:

'I am going to have a snooze. That Mr Luttrell said he would come this afternoon. If he comes you must entertain him, my dear. I'm exhausted.'

'Oh, I'm sure he won't come,' said Joan. 'He was very doubtful about it.'

Robert went to his sitting-room. Joan fetched her hat and a book and walked through the garden into the *podere*. Alexander Luttrell arrived at four. He was told by Robert's Italian servant that the Signore was resting and could not see anyone, and that the Signorina was out and would not be back till dinner-time. Alexander left two cards. Joan heard the bell of the villa clang. She would have given anything to have swallowed her pride, but it was too strong for her. She let him go without coming back to the house.

Directly Alexander got home he wrote her fully – a long letter – eight pages of passionate words in which he declared his love. The post seemed too slow for so important and sacred a message, and just before he left for the station he gave it to the porter, with a handsome tip, and told him to arrange for it to be sent by hand in a cab so that it would reach its destination that night. Had he sent it by post it would have probably reached Joan the next morning, or the next evening at the latest; as it was it never reached her at all. The hall porter put it aside meaning to see to it when his underling came in. Then, in the bustle of departing and arriving guests, he forgot all about it. He remembered it late that night and then, as it was too late to send it by hand, he posted it. The direction was – Villa Brendon, Maiano. Alexander, in his agitation, wrote rather indistinctly. Malano being read as Milano, it went to Milan. When it was returned, after some months, to the sender at the hotel, the members of the staff who received it, knowing nothing about it, put it in a pigeon-hole in case it should be called for, and there it remained.

Alexander had given Joan his London direction in the letter, and had said that if he did not hear from her he would understand that there was no hope for him. Her absence from home when he came to say goodbye had already made him suspect that this was the truth, because he did not believe that a mere change of plan on his part could have annoyed Joan to the extent of her not being willing to see him; and of course he knew nothing of Basil D'Eynecourt's gossip.

He had not been a week in England before the news of Robert Brendon's death at Florence was printed by *The Times* in the 'Deaths'. He had died suddenly from heart weakness brought about by a severe fit of asthma.

A few days later this was followed by another piece of news which concerned Joan.

This was the news of the death of Rowland Brendon, the grandson of Robert Brendon's great-uncle. As has been told, Joan's great-grandfather had left everything he could to a younger brother, and now came the news of the death of this grandson who had died childless at the age of thirty-three, of pneumonia. His property went to his next of kin – Joan.

Alexander Luttrell heard this last piece of news at his club, where Robert Brendon's brother-in-law, Horace Cantillon, had announced it to his acquaintances. He had heard nothing from Joan since his arrival in London. He suspected that he had made a mistake with regard to Joan's possible feelings, and yet at one moment he had felt sure that he had not.

In the meantime he had made up his mind that he would see no more of Mrs Dasent, whom he had left in Florence. He wrote Joan a letter of condolence, making no allusion to his former letter, and asking her not to answer; and she meant to acknowledge it promptly, but she did not do so; so his relations with Joan came to an end for the time being.

The Dasents returned to London and Mrs Dasent at once communicated with Alexander, complaining of his neglect and asking him to come and see her. This he did. She felt something had happened, but she was too wise and experienced to show it. She received him with complete friendliness, so everything went on as before.

Her father's death was no surprise to Joan; she knew her father had a weak heart, and the doctor had told her that any bad fit of asthma might now be fatal, yet when the blow did come her father's death seemed to her to be appallingly sudden. Robert had been sitting out in the garden in the afternoon – it was hot, and Florence was looking her loveliest. They dined together alone. After dinner he went to his room and went early to bed. No sooner had he gone to bed than he had a violent attack of asthma. He got up and sat in a chair. Joan gave him some medicine, but she was alarmed, and without her father knowing it she sent the carriage to Florence for the doctor. Robert dozed for a little, but in an hour's time he had another attack. The doctor arrived, but there was nothing to be done, and Robert died about ten minutes later. The doctor said that had he been there he could have done nothing. Robert was buried in the Protestant Cemetery at Florence. Aunt Amy came out for the funeral and wanted to take Joan back to England, but, as soon as the funeral was over, Joan, taking Kathleen with her, went to stay with Countess San Felice, and it was arranged that she should go to England to stay with her aunt in the autumn.

Joan would now have enough money to live independently, but she could not bear the thought of Florence without her father, so she determined to let or sell the villa as soon as she could and to let the country house she had inherited from her great-uncle. She stayed in Italy till the autumn with the San Felices, in Florence till the end of July, and then at a villa near Spezzia, where they went in August for the sea. At the end of September she went with Kathleen to London. During all this time she had heard nothing directly from Alexander Luttrell, and indirectly only once from her Aunt Amy, who said that she had thought at one moment he was attracted by her daughter Agatha.

'But,' she said, 'I was mistaken; he was occupied elsewhere.' She did not specify where.

Joan arrived in England at the end of September and went to her uncle's small country house in Surrey – 'Littlewood' – which was about half an hour from London.

CHAPTER 4

Joan's uncle, Colonel Horace Cantillon, was an MP for a London constituency. He was a handsome bearded man with a warm heart and an explosive vocabulary, violent at times, impatient always, easily angered, but no less easily appeased. His wife, Joan's Aunt Amy, had softness and charm, a great deal of her brother's humour without his pointed sharpness. She had soft eyes, dark hair, and there was about her an atmosphere of verbena and cherry-pie. She reminded one of a tea rose. Agatha, their eldest child, who was the same age as Joan, had her mother's softness and her father's warmth of heart; she was pretty, quiet and modest, her features were small, her eyes large and wistful, her manners exquisite, and her sympathy boundless. It was her first year out; mourning for her uncle's death had slightly delayed her entry into the world, but not long. He had died in April, and when two months had elapsed it was thought that she could go to balls with her Aunt Emily, Mrs Fausset, her father's sister, who was energetic and strong-willed and as busy as a bumble-bee.

Horace Cantillon, besides Agatha, had

four sons – all at school – and one small daughter who was still in the schoolroom.

It was impossible to be kinder than the Cantillons were to Joan, and she was instantly made to feel at home. Her Aunt Amy reminded her of her father; her Uncle Horace amused her and won her heart, and her cousin Agatha astounded her by her constant effacement and delicate unselfishness. In November the Cantillons were invited to –shire to stay at Saxon Court with Mr and Mrs Carleton, who had a shooting party that lasted a week.

Agatha and Joan were both invited. Joan had no wish to go, but saw no way of managing to refuse. A few days before they started, Mrs Cantillon heard from Mrs Carleton, who gave her a list of the guests, among whom were Alexander Luttrell and Colonel and Mrs Dasent. As soon as Joan heard that, she was determined not to go. As a child she had been used to pray when she was in any quandary to Childe Harold, her tortoise. She now, remembering her father and his sceptical tolerance of the saints, invoked St Anthony.

She could think of no reason why she should not go. But her petition was successful.

Time went on, but three days before they were to start Agatha and Joan were caught in the rain out driving in a pony-cart. The next day Joan was laid up with a severe cold and cough. The doctor said although it was nothing serious there would be no question of her getting up for a week. So it was settled she should stay behind with Mademoiselle and little Cicely, and the Cantillons telegraphed this to Mrs Carleton and started without her.

Mr Carleton had been for some years a barrister and subsequently a Member of Parliament. He married first an American, who died young leaving a large fortune but no children. He married again – this time the daughter of an impoverished landowner, the last representative of an important Whig family. He had retired from public affairs altogether, but he had a house in London as well as a country house. He was shy, hesitating and scholarly, and had translated the *Odes* of Pindar into English.

Four days after the Cantillons started, Joan, who was much better but was kept in bed by the doctor for fear she should get bronchitis, received a letter from Agatha. It ran as follows:

SAXON COURT
Wednesday

DEAREST JOAN,
I waited to write to you till I had been here a whole day so as to have something to say.

53

We arrived on Monday evening after a long but successful journey. Papa only made one scene at Eastham Station about the foot-warmers. We had sandwiches in the train. Saxon Court is a long way from the station, over an hour's drive. It is a very old house, done up lately and enlarged; it is very comfortable and Papa says the pictures are good. I have got a bedroom high up in a tower looking over the river.

The Carletons are very kind. Mr Carleton is quiet and gentle, with whiskers and an eyeglass. Papa *roars* at him every now and then. Mrs Carleton is rather shy and absent-minded and engrossed in *pottery* – baking pots in a kiln.

Geoffrey, the eldest boy, who has just left Cambridge, is here; the other two boys are at school. Janie, the only girl, is just out and rather shy, and there is a niece of the Carletons', Beatrice Lyle, who is taken out in London by Mrs Carleton. She has been out three years. Then there is a French couple, Monsieur and Madame de Neufchateau. They say they met you and Uncle Robert in Florence. There is a Lord Glencairn, a Scotch peer who has lived a great deal in Paris. Lord and Lady Castlebridge, a charming old couple with their daughter, Lady Fanny Morton, and her fiancé, Mr Tyne, good-looking, in the Diplomatic Service. He was in Florence this spring. They are going to be married in November. Then there is Colonel Dasent, who is deaf, and his wife, who is a beauty, and Mr Luttrell, who was one of my partners this summer. On Monday night I sat between Mr Luttrell and Mr Tyne. Mr Tyne talked all the time to his fiancée, and Mrs Dasent talked to Mr Luttrell till nearly the end of dinner, when her attention was claimed by Monsieur de Neufchateau, who was on her other side. After dinner there was whist for the old, and the rest of us played a game on the billiard-table.

The next day they went out shooting. We went to meet the shooters for luncheon and walked with them afterwards. Then home and tea. All the women in tea-gowns: Madame de Neufchateau's *lovely*. The older men went to the smoking-room. Janie and I had some music. At dinner I sat between Geoffrey Carleton and Lord Castlebridge.

I was less frightened than yesterday. Madame de Neufchateau wore a cream-coloured satin evening gown with glittering green and golden beetles on it.

Today Mrs Carleton is taking the women and the non-shooters – Lord Castlebridge, Mr Tyne and Geoffrey – for an expedition. The Dasents leave on Friday, the others all stay till Monday.

I do hope you are better, dearest Joan. We all miss you *very much*, and Mamma thinks you would have enjoyed it.

Your loving
AGATHA

Agatha had not observed a silent drama that was proceeding during this comfortable houseparty, of which she was the unconscious cause. Mrs Dasent was jealous of her. Alexander Luttrell had not talked to her much; but it was obvious that he thought her pretty, attractive and natural. He had not thought about her more than that. Joan was still in the background of his mind, and he felt certain that one day things would come right when they met again. He had made no break with Mrs Dasent, but he hoped that would settle itself. Mrs Dasent's instinct told her there was something wrong. Monsieur de Neufchateau admired her and she let him make up to her, hoping that it might make Alexander jealous, but to her great mortification he seemed delighted. She looked about for a cause of Alexander's tepidity, and came to the conclusion it was Agatha. She feared the young more than all. She was convinced Alexander would marry soon.

All her suspicions were suddenly increased and brought to a head by what happened next.

The morning after Agatha wrote her letter to Joan, on Thursday, it had been arranged that Mrs Dasent and Madame de Neufchateau were to follow the shooters: Mrs Carleton was taking the Castlebridges, Lady Fanny, Adrian Tyne, Janie, Agatha, Geoffrey and Beatrice for an expedition. At the last minute Alexander Luttrell, knowing that Adrian, who was a brilliant shot, was longing to shoot and show off before his fiancée and that there would only be six guns, said he would rather not shoot but go on the expedition.

So this was arranged: Adrian Tyne shot instead of Alexander, and Lady Fanny went with the shooters.

Mrs Dasent would have liked to have changed her mind at the last moment, but Monsieur de Neufchateau, who admired her, made it impossible.

So Alexander took part in the expedition. When he came back, and after they had all had tea and the guests had more or less dispersed, Mrs Dasent asked Alexander if he would very kindly fetch her book which she had left in the library, and before he had time to bring it back she followed him to that room, which nobody went to in the evening, and there matters culminated in a scene.

'I wanted to tell you,' she said, 'that Charlie and I are leaving tomorrow. Mother isn't well and wants to see me, and it's my only chance of seeing her, as on Monday we go to Norfolk for another week's shooting.

Now, as I shan't see you again for ages, I wondered whether you couldn't say that you'd been called back from here and come up on Saturday, and so we should have Sunday together in London.'

'They are shooting on Saturday and it would make them a gun short.'

'No, it won't, because I am leaving Charlie behind.'

'They'll still be a gun short.'

'Not if Adrian Tyne shoots instead of you.'

'Mrs Carleton has arranged for him and Lady Fanny to go to Mount Anselm, which belongs to her uncle.'

'Well, Geoffrey could shoot; he is longing to.'

'That wouldn't be fair; he can't hit a haystack.'

'You mean you won't come?'

'It's not that I don't want to, but I think it would be uncivil. Besides which, I think Charlie might think it odd.'

'Charlie is crazy about Madame de Neufchateau; he will think nothing.'

'I don't think I can. It would really be uncivil.'

'You mean you are quite determined to stay and flirt with Agatha Cantillon?'

'What nonsense!' Alexander turned a little red.

'Any fool could see that she's in love with you. Even Madame de Neufchateau noticed it, and you are encouraging her, and as I suppose you mean nothing I think it's a great shame.'

'That's all perfectly ridiculous.'

'Then why did you stay behind today and not shoot, and why did you go on the expedition? I hear you flirted with Agatha the whole time.'

'It was simply because Adrian Tyne was longing to shoot; you see, he's a wonderful shot; far better than I am.'

'Then why didn't Mr Carleton ask him to shoot instead of you?'

'I don't suppose he knew. Adrian has been abroad, and then he's younger than I am. I suppose they thought he'd like to spend all his time with his fiancée.'

'Well, what it means is this: that you have an opportunity of seeing me for once in a blue moon and you won't take it, although you know we shan't be able to see each other again for months.'

'Why not?'

'Because we are going to pay visits right up till Christmas, and for Christmas we are staying with Charlie's sister.'

'Oh, Hilda, do be reasonable; you know I should like to come.'

'I know you don't mean to. Why not be honest and admit what I have known ever since the summer, that it is all over? You are tired of me; you never want to see me again.

I have known this for some time. I knew what had happened, but I didn't know how it had happened. I was quite blind, poor fool that I was, although I saw you dance night after night with that girl and load her with cotillon presents!'

'I only danced the cotillon with her once at her mother's house.'

'Oh! How can you say that? I remember you dancing the cotillon with her at the Carletons'.'

'I had to. Mrs Carleton asked me to. I promise you I have never given her a thought.'

'You mean you have never given marriage a thought?'

'Oh, I suppose I shall marry some day.'

'Well, I'm glad to know. It had to happen some day and it's happened now. I hope you will be happy.'

'You shouldn't say such things, it's most unfair. Because I danced with somebody twice this summer. Why do you choose her more than anyone else? There are plenty of other girls I've danced with.'

'Oh, I know that: but you see women know these things at once. They know what counts and what doesn't.'

'As if I hadn't danced with you at every single ball we went to – besides the suppers.'

'Considering we used to be friends, that wasn't so very odd. However, if you come

60

up on Saturday I will forget all about it and say I made a mistake.'

'Hilda, I can't really; it would be too ridiculous.'

'You mean you think I am ridiculous? It's true. I know I am making myself ridiculous. I always have made myself ridiculous about you.'

'It's no good my saying anything. You twist everything I say. I promise you I have never given a thought to that girl; I think she's very nice.'

'I suppose you'll tell me you don't think she's pretty.'

'I think she's nice-looking.'

'That is kind of you.'

'There, you see. What is the good of our talking?'

'What indeed, when you are so sick to death of me that you can't even listen to what I say!'

'Hilda, really!'

'I knew it would happen this year. Do you know I thought it had happened when I saw you in Florence, and your sister told me she thought you were attracted by a girl who lived there. What is her name? Joan Brendon.'

Alexander turned crimson.

'Oh, this is too much!' he said. 'I won't be spied upon and badgered like that. I think it is intolerable.'

'Then it was true. That's why you wouldn't

speak to me in Florence. Alice said you could never marry her because she hadn't a penny. But now she's well-off – it makes it all the worse what you are doing here. It's not fair to Agatha.'

Alexander turned white with rage.

'I'm going,' he said.

'Very well, and understand,' she said, 'this time it really will be goodbye,' and she burst into tears.

At that moment they heard voices outside. She pulled herself together with extraordinary rapidity.

'Where is my book?' she said. They heard Madame de Neufchateau calling – 'Pierre, Pierre.'

She was about to open the door, but Monsieur de Neufchateau must have come from his bedroom on to the landing.

They heard his voice and then both voices speaking French as they went downstairs.

Mrs Dasent snatched a book from the table, left the room and went to her bedroom.

She did not sit next to Alexander that night. He was opposite to her, next to Agatha, and her jealous suspicions were confirmed.

Alexander himself felt as if someone had planted a new seed in his heart. Indeed it often happens that when a woman is jealous without a cause, the false cause with which she upbraids the man she loves becomes a real one, and it is her doing. She puts it into his head. She sows the seed.

Alexander thought Agatha more attractive than he had thought her before. He was blissfully happy.

Mrs Dasent, while talking hard to her neighbours, followed their conversation and suffered. 'It's all over. There's nothing to be done,' she thought.

The next morning she left for London.

CHAPTER 5

The Cantillons came home on the following Monday. They found Joan up and about, but she was not yet allowed to go out.

At dinner that evening nothing but the visit was discussed: the house; Mrs Cantillon said they had spoilt the rooms by unending protections against draughts.

'But that,' said Agatha, 'made the Neufchateaus happy. They said it was the first time they had been warm in an English house. Monsieur de Neufchateau said he could not understand *'la passion des Anglais pour les courants d'air'*.

'That confounded hot-water pipe,' said Colonel Cantillon, 'made the billiard-room like a hothouse.' There was one hot-water pipe in the large and lofty billiard-room, which in those days was considered a revolutionary innovation.

'Did the Neufchateaus enjoy it?' asked Joan.

'Yes, very much,' said Mrs Cantillon. 'They said they had met you at Florence.'

'Neufchateau is a very knowledgeable man. He shot very well and he appreciated the pictures.'

'And the food,' said Mrs Cantillon.

'Yes, Andrew's cook is good,' said Cantillon, 'and so is his claret.'

'It disagreed with your father, as usual,' said Mrs Cantillon.

'Oh! And Madame de Neufchateau's clothes! You should have seen them!' said Agatha. 'Green says she used to go to dress for dinner soon after tea; and she wore nothing complicated. It was all quite simple, but all just right. It made one despair.'

'Madame de Neufchateau is a handsome woman, but you looked just as well dressed as she did, dear child. I'm not sure you didn't look better.'

'Ah, those are the things no man ever notices, but we notice them,' said Mrs Cantillon with a sigh. 'She made me feel such a frump, and even Hilda Dasent, who does know how to dress, looked all wrong next to her.'

'Is she very pretty?' asked Joan.

'You should have seen her twenty years ago,' said the Colonel. 'Do you remember her, my dear,' he asked his wife, 'just after we married, at the Sussex House ball?'

'Yes,' said Mrs Cantillon, 'people stood on chairs to look at her complexion. Then she put on rouge and spoilt it all; but she's still a beautiful woman. Didn't you think so, Agatha?'

'Well, Mamma, if you ask me, I can quite

believe she has been lovely, but I was a little bit disappointed. I think she's got such colourless eyes, and her voice is ugly.'

'Yes, Agatha is right; her voice is common when she talks French. That did not prevent Neufchateau admiring her,' said Cantillon.

'And then there was an engaged couple, wasn't there?' asked Joan.

'Yes, Lady Castlebridge's girl, Fanny,' said Mrs Cantillon. 'Charming and *comme il faut*. She's going to marry Adrian Tyne. One can't help liking him, but I'm afraid he's reckless.'

'The Tyne blood,' said Cantillon, shaking his head.

Joan was longing to hear Alexander Luttrell mentioned, and yet fearful of his name being spoken. Agatha was in the same plight, and, feeling that danger to be imminent, she said hurriedly:

'It's the most comfortable house I have seen. There was a bathroom on my floor, and my room looked out on to a beautiful view: the woods and the river.'

'They've spoilt the house all the same,' said Mrs Cantillon. 'They've cut the gallery, which used to be lovely, into two rooms and made one of them a billiard-room.'

'They were right, my dear,' said Cantillon. 'It is more convenient as it is, and the pictures look well.'

The talk drifted to other things, and dinner was got through without Alexander being mentioned. They went to bed early, and, when they had said good night and gone upstairs, Agatha went to Joan's room to talk things over.

'Well, are you glad to be back?' asked Joan.

'Oh! It's such a relief! Although I did enjoy it – at least some of it. When I first arrived I thought it was going to be dreadful. The long drive from the station in a landau, and the first tea in the big hall, and Janie Carleton silent and *dying* of shyness just as I was, and then the terror of whom I should be next at dinner. But that turned out to be easy.'

'I forget whom you did sit next the first night.'

'I sat next to Mr Tyne, the diplomat who is engaged to Lady Fanny Morton. He's good-looking and great fun.'

'He was staying at Florence at Easter, but we didn't see him. But I suppose he was engrossed in his fiancée?'

'Oh! Yes...'

'And you had an old man on the other side?'

'No – Mr Luttrell.'

There was a pause.

'He was kind to me. You met him, didn't you, at Florence?'

'Yes. I met him at the San Felices'.'

'The Neufchateaus told us all about it. They said you spoke Italian like an Italian.'

'I ought to, as I lived there all my life. And

you didn't admire Mrs Dasent?'

'Oh, she *is* beautiful, of course, but I thought her rather affected. I liked him. He's a little deaf, but so civil.'

'But people *do* admire her, don't they?'

'I think Monsieur de Neufchateau did, but then Frenchmen are always so civil, aren't they, and always pay compliments? Every night I came down to dinner he said something to me about my toilette, even when I was only wearing my little grey, and he smothered Mrs Dasent with compliments. They know how to say that kind of thing without being ridiculous. It made Mr Luttrell laugh. He said even if it was a question of life and death he would not know how to say anything more than, 'What a pretty gown you've got on.' And that he would find difficult enough.'

'Is he amusing?'

'Oh yes, and quite easy: and sometimes he says things which are so funny in a serious way and people don't know whether he is being serious or not. Madame de Neufchateau never knew, but she thought it safe to laugh at everything he said in case she was meant to; so that if he said he hated racing, which he does, she treated it as a good joke.'

'Did everyone stay till Monday?'

'No, not everyone; Mrs Dasent went away on Friday. She had to go to her mother who was ill, and she left her husband behind.'

'And you liked the girl?'

'Who? Janie? Yes, she's an angel, and pretty. Mr Luttrell said she was like a Botticelli. But then he said that since he's been to Florence everyone looks to him like a Botticelli. He says Botticelli must have been an Englishman, as no Italian women are like his pictures.'

'Was there no other young man?'

'Nobody except Geoffrey Carleton.'

'And then there was someone else you wrote about.'

'Lord Glencairn?'

'Yes.'

'I thought he was frightening at first. He's rather fat, with small green eyes that twinkle, and reddish hair; but I found he wasn't frightening, really, but full of fun. He and Monsieur de Neufchateau talked French together. He has lived in Paris a great deal. Papa says he's got a large house in Scotland full of historical things that are priceless; but I believe he's a gambler and always in debt. In spite of his being supposed to be frightening and so much older he was easier to talk to than Geoffrey, for instance. He was charming to me and he showed me the pictures in the house. He knew the history of everything. Mr Luttrell said his grandfather was supposed to be the most good-looking man who ever lived, and that he died because he was rude to a gypsy who cursed him and the whole family, and said the head of the family would always die a violent death. His grandfather was run over and his father was drowned bathing.'

'Is he married?'

'Oh no.'

There was another pause.

'What did you all do Sunday?'

'We drove to church in the morning. Papa went to sleep during the sermon.'

'I suppose you didn't all go to church?'

'All the family and everyone, except the Neufchateaus, who are Catholics, and Lord Glencairn, who, Mr Luttrell said, was a strict Presbyterian, but that, of course, wasn't true.'

'And in the afternoon?'

'Some of us went for a walk: Mr Tyne, Lady Fanny, Geoffrey and I, and Janie and Mr Luttrell. Geoffrey and Janie took us to a sort of summer-house on the river. In the evening some of us acted charades and the rest were audience, as Mr Carleton doesn't allow whist on Sunday. Mr Tyne acted beautifully.'

'Did Mr Luttrell act?'

'No, nothing would make him. He was in the audience.'

'And did you act?'

'Oh! I did – but I had hardly anything to say. Madame de Neufchateau dressed us.

She did it so cleverly. She made Beatrice Lyle, who isn't pretty, look a beauty. Mr Luttrell guessed each syllable long before anyone else.'

'Is he clever?'

'I don't know, but he's very quick and he understands everything.'

'Well, you ended by enjoying yourself thoroughly.'

'Yes, I did, but I am glad to be back.'

Mrs Cantillon came into the room.

'You must let Joan go to bed, Agatha darling,' she said, 'because she isn't strong yet, and you too have had a tiring day.'

Good nights and a little talk at the door and then final good nights were said, and Agatha went to her room.

When Joan was left alone she said to herself:

'Agatha is certainly in love with Alexander; and I rather think he must be in love with her, because if not why did he stay behind when Mrs Dasent went away? Perhaps it was difficult, but if he had really wanted to go he would have found some excuse to go on Saturday. But perhaps he will be seeing her again directly. Whatever the situation may be, there is no hope for me – no hope.'

She remained awake a long time thinking, and the next day she looked tired, so much so that Mrs Cantillon noticed it and said she had been doing too much.

CHAPTER 6

The autumn went by and the Cantillons spent Christmas at Littlewood. Horace Cantillon's brother-in-law, Philip Fausset, and his wife Emily came for Christmas. Philip Fausset was a senior clerk in the Foreign Office. They had no children, and Mrs Fausset made up for the fact by managing the children of other people. As Joan had no parents, Mrs Fausset pounced upon her as a person to manage, and decided that she should make a good marriage, and that it should be her doing. Neither Joan nor Agatha could endure her. Horace Cantillon comforted himself by saying:

'Emily means well, but it's a pity she won't leave things alone.'

Mrs Cantillon bore her advice and her strictures in silence.

Emily Fausset was handsome. She had been painted by Winterhalter, and she had sparkling eyes and beautiful shoulders. She was untiringly energetic and she enjoyed saying that although her sister-in-law, dear Amy, had no will, she had enough for both.

After much discussion and cross-examination she felt certain that Agatha had a tender feeling for Alexander Luttrell, and that, she said, would do; whereas of course, Joan, being almost an heiress, must marry an older man who needed support of that kind. Alexander Luttrell's father, Lord Carhampton, was comfortably off. He had four sons and two daughters, and both the daughters were married. Mrs Fausset was determined to find a suitable husband for Joan, but at present she had not yet found what she considered exactly the right thing.

After Christmas the Cantillons went up to London, and this year Mrs Cantillon determined to take Joan out with Agatha

But matters were delayed. Joan caught typhoid fever soon after Christmas, and for six weeks she was seriously ill. When she was convalescent, Mrs Cantillon took her down to Brighton. By Easter, which they spent at Littlewood, she was well again and ready, Mrs Cantillon hoped, to face the London season.

The Cantillons had a small and comfortable house in Hill Street. The Carletons had a larger house in Belgrave Square. The first entertainment Joan went to in London was a dinner party at the Carletons', and there she met Alexander Luttrell for the first time she had seen him since Florence, and there also were Colonel and Mrs Dasent.

The breach which had been made in the relations between Alexander and Mrs

Dasent at Saxon Court had not been final. It had been mended; that is to say, it had been repaired, but in reality the mending was only superficial, for the damage was irreparable. Mrs Dasent knew this, but she clung desperately to the semblance and the shadow of what had been. She frequently told Alexander that he must of course marry, and that now was the time: if you married at all it was better to marry young. She had, so far, succeeded in making it impossible for Alexander to think of marriage.

Without any effort on his part or on hers, it happened that he was often thrown together with Agatha; and Mrs Cantillon in theory and Mrs Fausset in practice, under whose care Agatha went out during the period of Joan's illness, encouraged these meetings. So did Lady Carhampton, Alexander's mother, who was anxious for Alexander to marry; she deplored his infatuation for Mrs Dasent and thought Agatha would be an ideal wife for him. Thus it was they met at dinners and parties for the play. If Mrs Dasent had left the matter alone, all would have been well for her; he would have taken Agatha as a matter of course and not paid any real attention to her; but Mrs Dasent could not leave the matter alone. She made him a scene every time he met Agatha, and unconsciously she thus watered the seed she had sown, till it grew into a plant. Instead of seeing Agatha less on account of Mrs Dasent's displeasure, he saw her more. He wished, he said to himself, to prove to her, Mrs Dasent, how ridiculous she was being, and show he was independent and could not be bullied. The result was, Agatha fell in love with him. The matter became plain first of all to Mrs Fausset, and then to Joan, as soon as she was well, although Agatha had confessed and admitted nothing. This increased the resentment Joan felt towards Alexander, which had originally been caused by wounded pride. How did he dare, she said to herself, behave as he did towards girls; first towards herself and then to Agatha, when the whole world knew he was not free? Joan said such things to herself, but at the same time she wondered whether she was being perfectly honest; did she really believe that Alexander was irrevocably tied to Mrs Dasent? Was it reasonable to suppose such a thing? He was much younger than she was. Surely such things did not last for ever? But she always ended up when she went through this process of reasoning by saying to herself angrily: 'At any rate he's no right to behave like that, and it's not fair to Agatha.'

It was a large dinner at the Carletons'. Lord Stonehenge, the under-secretary for war, was there, and the Dasents, as well as the Cantillons. Just before dinner Lord

Stonehenge took Colonel Dasent aside and asked him whether he had made up his mind on the proposal which had been put before him.

'I will tell you after dinner,' said Colonel Dasent, who saw his wife approaching him.

Alexander took Joan in to dinner; on her other side was Lord Glencairn. Mrs Dasent was further down, at the other side of the table.

'We haven't met for a long time, you re-member,' said Alexander, 'not since Flor-ence.'

'No,' said Joan. 'Did you go there this year?'

'No. And you?'

'I have been in England all the winter and all the spring.'

'Yes, I heard about your illness.'

'From my cousin?'

'Yes. There is something I've always wanted to ask you,' said Alexander.

'Yes.'

'Did you get my letter?'

'Yes,' said Joan, thinking he meant his letter of condolence on her father's death, which was the only one she had had from him.

'You didn't answer it.'

'You asked me not to,' said Joan, 'but I meant to write all the same. It was very uncivil of me not to. I meant to, but...'

'Oh! not uncivil. There was nothing to say.'

'No, nothing; but I might have thanked you.'

'I understood.'

'After all, what is there to say? I know one could say nothing, but Papa used always to tell me I was uncivil.'

'I did really understand.'

'But you didn't; you thought I had been unfeeling.' Alexander laughed mirthlessly.

'Don't let's talk about it.'

'We won't, only I want you to believe I am sorry.'

'Let's talk of other things.'

But they didn't, because their conversation was interrupted. Alexander felt that he had now received the final answer to the letter he had written to Joan in Florence. He thought he had made a mistake, and there was no more hope of anything in that quarter, but he was just as much attracted by Joan as ever, and as he heard her talking and laughing with her neighbour, Lord Glencairn, he was tormented by jealousy. Joan felt no shyness with Glencairn. He was older, for one thing, and older people never made her shy, and she startled him by the things she said. She was different from the ordinary girls. They talked about theatres; Joan had only once been to a play in London.

'There is nothing worth seeing now,' Lord

Glencairn said. 'Later there will be the French play. Dorzan...'

'I should love to see her, but she is sure to act in plays that girls are not allowed to go to.'

'Why don't you go to a matinée, to the cheap seats, with your maid?'

'I'm too truthful – I couldn't take in Aunt Amy.'

'Well, all I can suggest is that you should get married.'

Joan was silent.

Lord Glencairn looked at her with an air of obvious appraisement and approval, and this made her feel more shy.

'It must be very interesting for you,' he said, 'to look at London from such a fresh point of view.'

'Is she pretty?' asked Joan, after a pause.

'Who? Dorzan?'

'Yes.'

'She can look prettier than anyone else if she wants to. She's not a beauty – like – well, Mrs Dasent, for instance.'

'I think she *is* beautiful.'

'Ah! you should have seen her twenty years ago.'

'That's what Uncle Horace says. But people admire her *now*, don't they? I should have thought nobody could help admiring her.'

Lord Glencairn saw that Joan was more

than normally interested, and wondered why.

At the same moment Alexander turned towards Joan, and Glencairn said, 'I think this is the prettiest dining-room in London,' and then left Joan to talk to Alexander, with whom she exchanged commonplaces.

While this conversation was going on, Mrs Fausset was discussing her nieces with Colonel Dasent.

'They are both here tonight, I see,' he said.

'I think they are both nice-looking, but there is really no comparison as to looks – your niece, Agatha, is a very pretty girl indeed.'

'I hope she will find a nice husband.'

'Have you anyone in view?'

'Nobody at present. We thought at one moment Alexander Luttrell was rather attracted by her, but, like all the young men nowadays, he won't look at girls.'

'That's because he's one of Hilda's slaves,' said the Colonel, laughing. 'It really is too bad; she's too old for that kind of thing.'

'She's looking too lovely, as usual,' said Mrs Fausset. 'It doesn't give the girls a chance.'

'Well, you needn't worry about that,' said the Colonel.

'Why?'

'You will hear soon enough.'

When the men were left together, Colonel Dasent went to sit next to Lord Stonehenge and said to him:

'I have quite made up my mind and I'm ready to go.'

'And your wife?'

'She will be delighted. I haven't told her yet.'

'Well, I'm glad,' said Lord Stonehenge.

When they went upstairs Alexander and Mrs Dasent sat in a corner of the drawing-room. There was a little music: some amateur singing, to which nobody paid much attention, except the songstress and the flustered accompanist.

Mrs Dasent had watched Alexander and Joan at dinner. Her instinct had enabled her to diagnose the situation correctly. Although she had made Alexander scenes about Agatha, she had dimly felt that he was not really in love with her. The danger was elsewhere, but where she did not know. Now she knew – she saw the whole thing. That accounted for the sudden change in his behaviour after Florence. Joan was more dangerous than Agatha. She was determined to put a stop to that.

'Did you enjoy your dinner?' she asked.

'I was next to Lady Hengrave, who always snubs me, and Miss Brendon, who hardly spoke to me.'

'That was Glencairn's fault; he was making himself unusually agreeable. He never talks to a girl as a rule. He must have been

81

attracted – she would attract him. She has always lived abroad, and he likes foreigners, and he knows foreign countries. I dare say they met in Italy. I expect he means to marry. She's well off. It would do beautifully.'

'If she liked him.'

'She does. There is no doubt about that. I talked to her after dinner. If he proposes she will accept at once.'

'He's much older than she is.'

'So much the better.'

'Would she like someone so much older?'

'Girls are infinitely more attracted by someone of an older generation than by a young man of their own. In the first place it is flattering to be noticed, and then the older people have seen things and known people and been everywhere, and can talk of interesting things, whereas the young can only say: "Are you going to Ascot?"'

'I suppose so. It doesn't sound to me natural.'

'That's because you're in love with Agatha.'

'I haven't said a word to her the whole evening.'

'That was not from not wanting to. You didn't get the chance. She is certainly pretty.'

'Well, I won't argue; it's no use.'

The music came to an end and the guests began to go.

As Colonel and Mrs Dasent drove home, Colonel Dasent told his wife he had been offered the post of Military Attaché at Washington. Lord Stonehenge, who was at the War Office, had asked him if he would take it.

'You refused, of course,' she said.

'No, my dear, I accepted. I think a change will do us both good.'

Mrs Dasent burst into tears.

CHAPTER 7

The summer went by swiftly for Joan. She was taken to a Drawing-room, to Ascot, and to the Queen's Ball.

She was on the whole not a success. Her aunt, Mrs Fausset, told her she did not take enough pains with her clothes, nor with the young men whom she took such trouble to ask to meet her. The only two men she had got on with were Alexander Luttrell and Lord Glencairn. But Alexander Luttrell was safely guarded till the Dasents left for America, which they did in July, and Lord Glencairn left London and went to Trouville in his yacht when the season of French plays came to an end.

Joan and Agatha were asked to stay in Scotland with Lady Alice Haslewood under the charge of Mrs Fausset. Agatha went, but Joan said she would prefer to stay with Mrs Cantillon at Littlewood. In the autumn the Countess San Felice paid them a visit and, hearing that the doctors said it would be unwise for Joan to spend the winter in England, she suggested that she should take Joan back with her to Florence. Joan accepted this invitation joyfully.

She stayed at the Villa San Felice till Easter, when the Cantillons came out with Agatha. They were going to Rome, and Joan joined them.

Directly the Cantillons arrived at Florence, Mrs Cantillon told Joan she had a surprise for her, but it was a dead secret at present.

'Agatha's engaged,' said Joan.

'Yes, she is,' said Mrs Cantillon, 'but we've told *no* one. Can you guess who it is?'

Joan could guess all too well, but she said: 'Is it Geoffrey Carleton?'

'No,' said Mrs Cantillon, 'it's Alexander Luttrell.'

'Oh! I am delighted,' said Joan. 'I may tell Agatha I know?'

'Yes, of course.'

And that evening Joan listened to the romance; the hopes, plans, despairs, reborn hopes, fresh plans and ultimate satisfaction that Agatha poured into her ear.

Alexander was coming out to meet them in Rome.

They stayed in Rome at an old-fashioned hotel.

Alexander Luttrell joined them at the hotel, and soon after their arrival they dined at the British Embassy. There they met Lord Glencairn, who was spending Easter in Rome. Joan sat next to him at dinner, and once more found she could talk to him without any shyness, and with perfect ease. He told her that Dorzan was giving a few farewell performances. He had a box for the next two nights and he was going to ask all her party.

'But I shan't be allowed to go,' said Joan.

'Surely in Rome. I thought those rules only applied to London.'

'My father didn't mind my seeing anything,' said Joan, 'but even he wouldn't have taken me to the play if he knew it would shock other people, and then there's Agatha; she's seen nothing, and Uncle Horace would never let her go to a play that isn't *pour les jeunes filles.*'

'Well, as a matter of fact it is.'

'What, the play?'

'Yes. It might have been chosen for you. It is Musset's *On ne badine pas avec l'amour.* It's true she's doing a one-act play by Dumas Fils first, which would indeed *not* do: but we'll miss that.'

'Oh! Musset. Papa was so fond of him. We often read his plays.'

'Well, I shall arrange that with your uncle.'

The subject was broached after dinner, and Mrs Cantillon, after consulting the Ambassador and a Princess Roccapalumba, a beautiful Englishwoman married to an Italian who was an invalid, agreed they might all see the Musset, provided that they missed the first play, which was *impossible.* So the following night they arrived at the Argentina in the long entr'acte and they were told by Lord Glencairn, who met them, that Dorzan had just achieved a personal triumph, but the audience had jibbed at the one-act play, and there had been some hisses.

'It has made her nervous,' he said, 'but she will act all the better for that. She says she always acts her best when she feels there is something to fight.'

Anaïs Dorzan had had a strange career. Her mother was a Spaniard, and her father belonged to a good French family. She had been brought up in a convent and had at first wished to become a nun, but she had suddenly been seized by a vocation for the stage. She had studied at the Conservatoire and become a *pensionnaire* at the Comédie Française. She had not been successful at first; the parts she was cast for didn't suit her. She had decided to leave the stage, when, owing to the illness of a well-known actress, she had to play Camille in *On ne badine pas avec l'amour*. This part brought her fame, and from that moment she never looked back, and played important parts in high comedy and drama.

After the war in 1870 she decided that modern drama was her speciality, and for this the Comédie Française did not give her sufficient scope. She went abroad, to Italy, where she was triumphant in many cities, to Russia and to London, where the same thing happened, and then back to Paris at one of the theatres on the Boulevard.

When she was in Italy an Italian nobleman, Alfredo Chiaromonte, fell in love with her and became her lover; but when she left Italy she suddenly and finally left him and refused to see him again. Nobody knew why – she was said to be desperately unhappy. There appeared to be no rivals. Then she announced, after having made a fresh sensation in a drama by a new author, that the stage was killing her and that she could act no more. She consented to make a tour in Italy, for which she was under contract, and that should be her farewell – these performances in Rome should be the last before she said goodbye to the stage for ever.

Glencairn had often seen her act in Paris and had assisted at her first triumphs before the Prussian War, but it was not until after the war and after her return from Italy and Russia that he made her acquaintance. It was with Anaïs as a private person off the stage that he fell in love, not only madly and violently, but so thoroughly that he wished to make her his wife. This was in the summer, the preceding year (1874). She was at Dieppe, and he went there in his yacht. She told him she had decided to leave the stage, which was killing her. What could be better, he urged, than for her to marry him? They would live in whatever country she liked. Then, just when he hoped for an ultimate consent – although she had never said anything to justify his hopes – she told him that she could never love any man. She had decided to leave not only him but the world, and to enter a convent, which indeed had been her earliest vocation.

This had happened in the autumn. She convinced Glencairn that she meant it, and that all was over; and now he had come to Rome to see her last performances.

She was leaving the stage and the world at the height of her fame. She had conquered Europe and received fabulous offers to go to America, but she said, and perhaps rightly, that the stage was killing her.

Anaïs Dorzan was not a tragedian; unlike Rachel, she left classic parts alone, as well as the romantic poetic drama whose heroines Sarah Bernhardt was soon to interpret so divinely. Her poetry was the prose of life, and in her hands it turned to fire.

She was not tall, but slim, supple and slight; she had the body of a waif. She was not pretty, but much more – her face was infinitely intelligent and could express anything. She could *act* beauty, great beauty. Her eyes were wide apart, round and sad. When she was angry you saw no white – they were all black, like, people said, the eyes of the devil. Her features were small and short – her head small, with light brown curly hair correctly curled according to the fashion of the day, and poised on a lovely neck. She had a strange voice, a little nasal, with a tang in it. At first you were not sure whether it was pleasing, and then you were caught by its delicate halftones, and after a time it was irresistible; ravishing; sheer magic. There was nothing she could not express, from the ringing laugh of a tomboy to the wild cry of despair of a hunted animal; and then in her soft passages there was a thrill in her voice, something bitter-sweet and infinitely sad that melted the heart and gave you cold shivers, like a violin played by a great artist, or the flute of a faun or the Pipes of Pan. She made you laugh or cry as she pleased. She intoxicated an audience, and could excite it to a frenzy of passion and sorrow or to an ecstasy of delight. Musset's Camille, in that delicate poem of a play, was the part, although it did not afford her scope for the full range and gamut of her powers, in which her art seemed most consummate. She made the passion – the suppressed passion – the stifled pride, ring so true. She expressed in it all the thwarted and baffled desire of all unhappy lovers, quietly, simply and rapidly.

She seemed to make no effort; she underlined nothing; and yet she expressed everything. Her playing was full of overtones:

every gesture, every look meant something: everything seemed fresh, new and un- expected, and yet things happened a little too quickly for you to notice how they had happened. You were carried straight on the whole time. Sometimes her eyes seemed as hard as precious stones, and sometimes like pools reflecting an immense far-off sorrow; and when she smiled it was like sunshine on a field of bright flowers.

After the second act, Joan was swept off her feet. Colonel Cantillon cried; Agatha and Alexander were spellbound; Lord Glencairn looked on with a sullen expression.

'Don't you think she is wonderful?' Joan asked him in the entr'acte.

'Oh, she can act!'

The audience – accustomed to chatter – listened in silence, and shrieked themselves hoarse at the end of the second act.

'You know her?' Joan asked Lord Glencairn.

'Oh yes; well,' he laughed a little drily.

'Shall you go round and see her?'

'Not tonight. There will be ever so many people without me,' he said, rather grimly.

In the last act, in the scene where she throws herself on the prie-dieu and implores heaven not to abandon her, she swept the house off its feet, and at the close of the play the audience gave her an ovation such as only Italians are capable of, and smothered her with garlands of flowers, and called her before the curtain till she could come no more.

'Won't you go and congratulate her?' Joan asked Glencairn.

'Not tonight,' he said. 'I will find you my carriage.'

He had noticed that Alfredo Chiaromonte was in the audience.

Joan drove home with her aunt and uncle in silence. She felt that the door of a new world had been opened for her.

'I understand why she is leaving the stage,' she said. 'One couldn't possibly go *on* acting like that night after night.'

'The poor child,' said Colonel Cantillon. He was still crying.

'It's a very sad play,' said Aunt Amy, 'but I'm glad you've seen her; it will be something, for you girls to tell your children.'

A few days later Agatha's engagement was announced in *The Times*. During the whole of their stay in Rome Lord Glencairn came to see them every day. He was, Colonel Cantillon said, very civil. He lent them his carriage; he took them to the Campagna, to Tivoli and Frascati, to many private picture galleries. Agatha and Alexander naturally spent all the time they could together, and Lord Glencairn devoted his whole attention to Joan. They did not go to the French play again, as Dorzan had only acted in plays that the girls were not allowed to see, and then Dorzan left Rome. Lord Glencairn introduced them to several of his Roman friends.

They were to break their journey on the way home at Florence. The day before they left, Lord Glencairn had organised an expedition to Hadrian's Villa, where they spent the day; while Colonel and Mrs Cantillon were resting in the shade, and Agatha and Alexander had disappeared in one direction, Lord Glencairn led Joan in another, and, after they had talked a little about her immediate plans, Joan thanked him for his great kindness, for having taken so much trouble about them, and she ended by saying, 'We shall miss you.'

'But we shall meet again soon in the summer. I am coming to London.'

'London is so different,' said Joan.

'Need it be different?'

'I don't know. I only know it is.'

'It depends on you.'

'What do you mean?'

'It depends on you not to make it different.'

There was a silence.

'I mean, if you choose there is no reason why we should ever separate – if you will be my wife.'

Joan was surprised, and yet not surprised. A thousand thoughts passed through her brain in a flash. She felt she liked him better than anyone she had ever met. She knew she did not love him, as she could have loved Alexander, but then she also knew she would never love anyone as she might have loved him. She felt she would never love anyone better than she could love Lord Glencairn; she felt she would prefer him to anyone as a husband.

'I thought you loved Dorzan,' she said spontaneously. Nobody had ever mentioned the subject to her.

'I did. I did love her madly, but that has all been over for a long time – at least, it never really began. It never came to anything, but I was like a man who was dazed, and now I have come to.'

'Won't it begin again?'

'Oh no.'

'I should think Dorzan could do anything with anybody, if she chose.'

'She's going into a convent; she's going to be a nun; she always wanted to.'

'I don't think you had better risk it,' said Joan.

'Say yes,' he said in a whisper.

'When I say yes,' she said, 'I mean it; are you sure? Do you want me to?'

'I have wanted you to from the first moment I set eyes on you. You *know* that.'

'Well, yes,' said Joan.

Joan told her aunt what had happened that evening, and Mrs Cantillon told her husband. Mrs Cantillon was delighted; Colonel Cantillon was not so sure. Glencairn had the name of a *viveur* and a spendthrift, and somewhat of a rake.

'And they make the best husbands,' said Mrs Cantillon.

They agreed there was really nothing they could object to, and it was settled that it should be announced when they got back to London. Joan, of course, told Agatha. They were to stop two nights in Florence on their way home, and a few days in Paris to get clothes. Alexander was with them, but Lord Glencairn had been obliged to go straight home to London. Agatha had caught a bad cold just before they left Rome. After the journey it was distinctly worse, and Mrs Cantillon thought it wiser that she should stay one day in bed, as she had a slight temperature.

They were to drive in the afternoon to the Villa Brendon, where Joan had lived with her father. The villa had been let all through the winter, but the tenants had left. Joan wanted to see the servants. It was agreed that Agatha, who was in bed, would be the better for being left quietly to herself, and they drove off to the villa after luncheon.

As they were leaving the hotel, Alexander asked the hall porter whether there were any letters for him, as he was expecting to hear from his sister. He had not heard from her since his engagement had been announced.

'There are no letters,' said the hall porter.

'Are you sure?' asked Alexander. 'Just look. There should have been a letter waiting for me.'

He had asked his sister to write to Florence.

The hall porter pulled out the letters which were in the pigeon-hole 'L' and went through them, showing them to Alexander.

'You see, Signor, there is nothing.'

'What about that one?' He had pointed to one on which he seemed to recognise his own handwriting.

'Oh, that has been here nearly two years. It was sent back.' The porter looked contemptuously at the envelope that was covered with crossed directions and redirections.

'Let me look,' said Alexander. He took his letter and said, 'Yes; that is for me.'

It was the letter he had written to Joan two years ago, and which had been to Milan and back. The hall porter burst into a torrent of explanations.

'This letter,' said Alexander, 'I left to be sent off when I was here two years ago, and it has been returned to me. It doesn't matter.'

He put the letter in his pocket.

They drove to the Villa Brendon, where they were warmly welcomed by the old caretaker and his wife, who were overjoyed at seeing Joan, and insisted on opening all the shutters and suggested making tea. But Joan, knowing their idea of tea, made signs to her aunt, who said they must be home for tea. They sat for a while on the verandah, looking at the view.

'There is a better view from the *podere* up on the hill,' said Joan; 'that used to be my favourite spot. I think I must see it.'

'We will wait here, my dear,' said Mrs Cantillon. 'I don't think we could manage that climb.'

'Well, I won't be long,' said Joan, and she started walking down the steps.

'May I come with you?' asked Alexander.

'Of course,' said Joan.

They walked up the hill in silence; when they got to the top they turned round and looked at the view.

'It's a lovely view,' said Joan, 'isn't it? I am going to sit down for a moment.'

They both sat down.

'Do you remember,' said Alexander, 'my asking you in London when we met at dinner at the Carletons' if you had got my letter?'

'Yes, after my father's death.'

'That was the letter you meant; but it wasn't the letter I meant.'

'What do you mean?'

'I mean that two years ago when I was at Florence, the day I left I came to see you to say goodbye, and you were out.'

Joan said nothing.

'You were not at home, at any rate.'

Joan still said nothing.

'I had to leave Florence that night, but before I left I wrote you a letter. I asked the hall porter to send it by hand. It wasn't the same hall porter as there is now. I suppose he forgot; anyway it was posted, and instead of going to Maiano it went to Milano, and I don't know then what happened to it. Then it came back to Florence and I found it waiting for me. I had left no direction behind me there. I was expecting nothing, and I had told you my London direction in my letter.'

'How odd. You must have thought me uncivil, especially as I didn't answer your second letter.'

'I asked you *not* to answer the first letter unless...'

'Unless?'

'Unless the answer was *'yes'*. I asked you to marry me.'

Joan turned white. Neither of them looked at the other.

'Supposing you had got the letter?'

'Don't let us talk about it. What's the use? It's all too late.'

'Is it?'

'You know it is.'

'Not if – we still feel–'

'It's too late, whatever we feel. You have promised to marry Agatha. It will break her heart if you don't.'

'And you have promised to marry Glencairn.'

'It wouldn't break his heart if I didn't, but I said I would and I mean to keep my word.'

'You don't love him.'

Joan said nothing.

'Aren't we being cowardly? Wouldn't it be better to tell the truth? I love you and you know it, and you love me and I know it, and nothing can or will change that. Wouldn't it be more honest as well as more sensible to say so instead of each of us–'

'Very few people marry those whom they *love*.'

'But when there *is* the chance–'

'It would kill Agatha. Nothing would make me marry you now – nothing, nothing. And what right had you to ask me then – when–'

'When what?'

'When all the time there was someone else.'

'Hilda? That was all over. It had been all over for a long time. You know that is true. You know that whatever there had been in my life – everything from the first day we met at the San Felices', and then again at the Uffizi, and then again at the picnic – was different. You know that, and if I could have seen you again – if you hadn't been out that afternoon–'

'I wasn't out. I was here, where we are now,

100

and in the garden. I heard you ring the bell, but I was angry. A man came to luncheon on Sunday and talked of you and Mrs Dasent. He said you adored her, and that you ran after anyone. I knew that wasn't true, but I was jealous and angry, and too proud to see you when you came.'

'Must we make a mistake a second time? Now that we have been given the opportunity of putting it right?'

'Agatha–'

'Wouldn't she get over it?'

'No, never. She is the gentlest, most delicate thing in the world. She is far better than you or than me. She is far too good for you – too good for anyone.'

'Then have I the right to marry her?'

'You have no right to marry anyone else. You will be very happy.'

'I think we are being cowardly.'

'I think it would be cowardly to do anything else.'

'Very well. I will tear up the letter I wrote you.'

'Tear it up; and now we must go back. They will be wondering why we are so long.'

They walked down in silence to the garden.

'Go up to the house,' said Joan; 'I want to speak to the gardener.'

She found the gardener, and a short talk with him gave her time to compose herself.

Then she walked back into the house.

'How charming the villa is,' said Mrs Cantillon, 'and how nice to think that if you should ever want to come to Florence you can come here.'

'I am fond of it, of course,' said Joan.

'It will be a charming place for your honeymoon,' said Colonel Cantillon.

CHAPTER 8

Alexander and Agatha were married towards the middle of June in London. Alexander had been offered the appointment of Military Secretary to the Governor of Madras, who was a friend of his father, and it was settled that he and Agatha should sail for India in the autumn, after spending their honeymoon and the last of the time that remained to them in England at Lord Carhampton's house in the country. Joan and Lord Glencairn meant to be married soon afterwards quietly at Littlewood. They were to go to Paris for their honeymoon, and then to Naples before settling down at Glencairn Castle in the island of Travistacore, on the west coast of Scotland.

Joan was bridesmaid at Agatha's wedding. Her aunt, Countess San Felice, was living with her daughters at her brother-in-law's flat in Paris and had come over to London for the wedding, and she suggested that as Joan was going to spend her honeymoon in Pans, and as they wished the wedding to be quiet – Lord Glencairn had no relations living except a sister who had married a Russian and lived in the Crimea – she should come over to Paris and stay with her, and be married there from her flat. Her Uncle Horace and her Aunt Amy, who were going to take the waters at Vichy, could stop in Paris on the way. This was arranged, and Joan went to Paris with Countess San Felice directly after Agatha's wedding. A few days later they received the news that Horace Cantillon's horse had run away with him in Rotten Row. He had been thrown and had broken two ribs and a collar-bone. This made it impossible for the Cantillons to come to the wedding.

They were married in a little church which was in the same street as Countess San Felice's flat. Joan was given away by Pietro San Felice. The only people who attended the wedding were Joan's Aunt Mabel and her daughters, Dr Maclean, who was Glencairn's best man, and Kathleen. It was a matter of indifference to Joan and to Glencairn whether they were married in a Catholic or a Protestant church, but Countess San Felice told them that it was Maria Brendon's dying wish that Joan should be married in a Catholic church: besides this, Joan knew that Kathleen would never get over it if she were married anywhere else.

The night before the wedding Glencairn and Dr Maclean dined together at the Café Anglais.

Dr Maclean, talking of the marriage

service, asked Glencairn what religion the children would be brought up in.

'If I ever have any children,' he said, 'and the fortune-tellers, who are always right, say that I shan't, they shall be brought up as Protestants. Joan doesn't care. She is being married in a Catholic church to please her aunt, who, like all Italians, is superstitious, but, after all, not more superstitious than I am.'

After the wedding, there was a breakfast in the apartment on the entresol of the Hôtel Bristol, which Glencairn had taken for the honeymoon. It was attended by the San Felices and Dr Maclean, who proposed the health of the bride and bridegroom.

When the breakfast, which lasted some time, was over, Glencairn left Joan with her aunt to unpack her things, and said he was going out for a little stroll. He would be back in the evening and they would drive to the Bois and have dinner out of doors. He strolled down the Rue de Rivoli, bought Galignani's newspaper at a kiosk, and then walked up the Avenue de l'Opéra to the boulevards, stopped at the first café he came across, and sat down at a table in the street and ordered some coffee.

As he glanced at the column in his newspaper which announced the arrivals and departures at the hotels in Paris he caught the name of the 'Count and Countess

Chiaromonte', who had arrived at the Hôtel Meurice.

'I wonder who his wife is,' he said to himself, 'and when he was married.'

After he had sat for over an hour at the café watching the passers-by – it was a lovely July day, and Paris, although said to be empty, was still full of people – he walked down the Avenue de l'Opéra till he got to the Théâtre Français, and he had the curiosity to go and see what they were giving that night. It was *Phèdre*, with that new actress, Mademoiselle Sarah Bernhardt, playing the chief part. As he read the names on the poster, he was conscious that someone else was doing the same thing; he turned round and found himself face to face with Anaïs Dorzan. She looked pale and thin, but she was beautifully dressed.

She smiled at him and said:

'What a happy meeting! I hear you are going to be married.'

'I am married; I was married this morning.'

'All my best congratulations. They say she is charming.'

'I was just on my way back to the hotel,' he said. 'Joan is unpacking, and she has her aunt with her. Let us walk together as far as the Tuileries Gardens. There are several things I want to ask you.'

Dorzan looked at her watch.

'Very well,' she said, 'but it is getting late and I can't stay long. Tell me all about your wife.'

Glencairn told her all he knew of Joan's history, and they talked lightly, like old friends, till they reached the Tuileries Gardens and sat down on a seat.

'And you, Anaïs,' he then said, 'you have left the stage?'

'Oh yes, for ever!'

'But you have not gone into a convent,' he said, slightly ironically.

'I changed my mind,' she said.

'The last time we met you seemed sure of it.'

'I *was* sure of it. Some day I think it may still happen. I was going to write to you today. I saw in the newspaper you were at the Bristol, and all about your marriage, but now it isn't necessary. I too am married. I was married a fortnight ago in Rome. It has been kept secret. I did not want the *réclame*, but it will soon be known now.'

'Not to–'

'Yes – Alfredo Chiaromonte.'

'Then all that story about the convent was–'

'Perfectly true.'

'But you found you loved him too much after all.'

'I don't love him.'

'Then why?'

'I can't explain; you would never understand. Nobody could ever understand.'

'You might have told me.'

'What difference could it have made?'

'All the difference.'

'I would never have married you.'

'If you could marry Alfredo Chiaromonte you could have married me, as you say you don't love him.'

'He was the only man I could marry. You must believe me; it is useless to ask me why. It is like that. And, after all, what have you to complain of, since you are married?'

'Do you think I would have married if I had known? Do you think I could ever love anyone as I loved you – as I *love* you? My married life is over from today. It will never begin.'

'Do not say such silly things.'

'You know they are not silly. Oh, Anaïs, how could you do such a thing? How could you not tell me? And I believed you. I believed *in* you.'

'It was all true: but, believe me, I should never have married you.'

'But what made you marry Alfredo? You say you don't love him.'

'He was the only man I could marry; I can't explain. It is too difficult – too complicated. It was my only safety. That or the convent. The convent would have been better, but I let Alfredo persuade me. You see, he has always loved me, long before I knew you. He was more than a lover to me. He was a friend – a saviour.'

'From what?'

'Ah! from myself.'

'How could you? How could you?'

'I must go home. Alfredo is at the club, but he is coming to fetch me.'

'And I must go home – to my wife. Anaïs, you have made a mistake – a great mistake. I could have made you happy. I would have lived wherever you liked. You could have gone on acting if you had liked.'

'Never, never, never. You don't understand, and I can't explain, so what is the use? I am an unhappy woman. You must believe me: but I don't think I shall live long, fortunately. That is one reason why I married Alfredo. Acting killed me, and it is too late for me to recover.'

'Oh, what nonsense! I don't believe you are telling me the truth.'

'I swear I am. I swear it by everything I hold most sacred. You must pity me. You mustn't be angry with me. It couldn't be otherwise. You must make your wife happy.'

'My wife! She shall never be my wife now.'

'What difference does it make? If you could marry when I was going into a convent, why can't you be happy married now that I am married to someone else?'

'How can you ask such questions? Is it *you*

109

asking such questions? *You*, who have expressed the innermost secrets of the torture of jealousy, and the whole frenzy of love? Don't you see that now I have seen you again, and that you belong to someone else, it is all different and impossible? I shall never be able to look at Joan.'

'Poor child, you will ruin her life.'

'As you have ruined mine. It's your fault.'

'I always told you the truth. I always told you I could never love you – never belong to you. I never lied to you.'

'Except about the convent.'

'But it was true *then*. I meant it; but it would have killed Alfredo, and if you knew what he was to me in the past... I couldn't act differently. Try to believe I am telling you the truth.'

'How can I, when I know what a consummate actress you are?'

'Oh, that isn't true. I have never acted in real life; never play-acted either to Alfredo or to you. You know that is true, don't you?'

'When you talk like that I would believe anything, and I do believe it; but when your life with Alfredo comes to an end – and it will come to an end – I shall be waiting for you.'

'Goodbye, my poor friend,' she said, getting up. 'Believe me, you cannot be as unhappy as I am. My whole life has been one great mistake; and there is no remedy for it but death, which I hope may come soon. Goodbye, my poor friend.'

She walked away.

Lord Glencairn stayed behind, walking up and down the garden like one demented. Then he looked at his watch, called a cab, and drove to the hotel, where he found Joan waiting in an elegant 'going-away' gown and bonnet.

'We will drive to the Bois,' he said. 'The carriage is waiting for us downstairs, when you are ready.'

They had not been driving for many minutes before Joan saw that something had happened.

'Is anything the matter, Ian?' she asked.

'Yes,' he said, 'I have had a telegram from Glencairn, from the factor. We shall have to go home at once. It is a question of the sale of some land which can't be settled till I am on the spot.'

It was true he had received such a summons, but there was no immediate hurry, and had matters been otherwise he would not have obeyed it.

He pointed out the objects of interest to her, and sometimes an acquaintance or a celebrity.

They drove to a café which was far out in the Bois, and Glencairn chose a table under the tall trees and ordered dinner.

Joan saw that something had happened to

him. He looked ten years older.

They had dinner in silence.

When the coffee came and Glencairn lit his cigar, he said:

'I'm sorry to be like this.'

'You're not well?'

'No, I'm not well. I'm ill – incurably ill.'

'What is it? Don't tell me, if you don't like.'

Glencairn buried his face in his hands.

'You'd better know. You'll have to know some day. You had better know at once. I have seen her again.'

'Dorzan?'

'Yes – she's not gone into a convent; she's married.'

'And if you had known that,' said Joan, 'you would not have married me.'

Glencairn said nothing.

'She's married Alfredo Chiaromonte,' he said presently. 'She'd told me *that* was all over. She swore everything was all over; that she was leaving the world for ever.'

'She probably meant to.'

'What does it matter what she meant? She didn't; she hasn't.'

'I knew the risk was too great. I knew this might happen,' said Joan. 'It is my fault; I had no right to marry you. You belonged to someone else. We must make the best of it. You can trust me to keep up appearances. Nobody will ever know. You must take me to

Scotland and leave me there, and then you can do what you like. I am fond of the country and I am used to being alone.'

'I'm very sorry,' he said. 'I ought to be shot.'

'We each of us made a mistake,' said Joan. 'I always knew I had no right to marry you. I am every whit as much to blame as you are.'

'You are very noble,' said Glencairn, with a dry laugh; but he meant what he said, and his bitter laugh was against himself. Joan thought the irony was directed at her; she too had meant what she had said, but the reason why she felt that she had done wrong in marrying Glencairn was not that he had loved Dorzan but that she loved Alexander Luttrell.

She was now stung by what she thought was his irony, and too deeply wounded to speak. She turned to ice. After he had paid the bill she followed him out of the restaurant. Glencairn made a few remarks; Joan answered icily. They drove to the hotel in silence – almost total – and when they got up to their sitting-room Glencairn took up a newspaper.

Joan said 'Good night, Ian; I hope you will be better tomorrow.'

Then she went through his small bedroom and dressing-room into her large bedroom and shut the door, and sitting in front of her dressing-table she silently cried till she could cry no more. Glencairn stayed in the sitting-room and read *The Times* and smoked a cigar.

Then, looking at the clock and seeing it was nearly twelve, he went downstairs and walked into the Place Vendôme, where he took a cab and drove to a small restaurant which in old days he used to frequent. He was not hungry. He didn't want to go home, but he didn't want to do anything else. He sat down at a table, when someone sitting on the opposite side of the restaurant beckoned to him. It was Jules Dalmain, the author of a play in which Dorzan had acted with success. He had met him with her. He was now having supper with an actress. Glencairn walked over to his table and Dalmain asked him to join them, introducing him at the same time to his companion. Dalmain, who lived entirely in the literary world and took no interest in anything beyond or outside it, knew nothing of what had happened to Glencairn.

Glencairn sat down at their table and ordered a bouillon. Dalmain at once plunged into a complicated narrative of the fortunes and vicissitudes of his new play, which had been accepted by the Théâtre Français and then rejected, and now accepted by the Gymnase, and which he expected to have produced in September.

He told Glencairn a long story of cabals and intrigues of which he had been the victim: how a rival dramatist and a rising actress had conspired together to bring about the refusal on the part of the director of the Théâtre Français to produce his play, after it had been unanimously accepted at the reading.

'But,' he said, 'I no longer care a rap. I shall have a better cast and a better audience, and they will be sorry.'

Glencairn asked him what the play was about, and Dalmain told him the plot in great detail; his companion did not interrupt, but every now and then she said:

'*That* scene is a marvel.'

Then Glencairn asked who was going to act in it, and this started Dalmain on another long story about the choice of the cast.

Blanche Sabine was going to play the principal part. 'Jeanette,' he said, pointing to his companion, 'is playing the ingénue. It is her first big part.'

'And a very difficult part too,' said Jeanette, 'perhaps the most difficult part in the play.'

'Of course,' said Dalmain, 'the chief part was really written for Dorzan.'

'She's given up the stage, hasn't she?' asked Glencairn carelessly.

'Yes, for marriage!' said Dalmain, and he

laughed sardonically.

'Really! And who is her husband?' asked Glencairn.

'An old love of hers, an Italian. It hasn't lasted long.'

'Really?'

'He is upstairs in this restaurant at this very moment, having supper in a *cabinet particulier* with *des filles*. She ought never to have left the stage, but she will come back, and if she does I will write her something first-rate. You see, in this play I am doing now, in the first act the public must *feel* that the man really thinks he has given up the woman for ever – when she tells him it is all over, and that she has given up everything and is leaving the world. He is sincere and means to make a good husband, but when he finds the other woman has married someone else, then his old love comes back a hundredfold more strong and he is determined to get her again, and his wife no longer exists for him. Do you think that situation very improbable?'

'Not at all,' said Glencairn. 'It's the kind of thing that might easily happen in real life.'

CHAPTER 9

Joan and her husband went straight back to Scotland. They stayed a night in London and Joan saw her Aunt Amy and told her she was happy. They were given a tremendous welcome at Travistacore. They arrived there on board Glencairn's steam yacht the *Firefly*, and they drove to the castle through triumphal arches, and were greeted with deputations and addresses.

Glencairn Castle was a large white building with turrets, set high on the top of the hill, and in front of it were terraces which went right down to the sea. It was, thought Joan, like a castle in a fairy tale. Inside it was furnished in a comfortable early Victorian fashion. There was a great deal of tartan and a great many stags' heads hung on the walls; there were some fine pictures, and the glass cabinets were full of historical relics.

Glencairn was fond of yachting and spent a great deal of time on board his yacht. Joan was a bad sailor, and he only took her when it was smooth.

In August he asked some people to shoot, and they often had visitors who came for a day or two. Joan made friends with the local

117

inhabitants and liked them, and they liked her.

Joan went to London to say goodbye to Agatha when she sailed for India in September, and stayed with her aunt. Agatha was radiantly happy. At Christmas, Glencairn asked the Cantillons to stay with him, and the house was full of people. Joan stayed in Scotland until the following Easter. Her husband made frequent visits to London – he was on Boards in the City. After Easter he suggested she should go to London with him. He had a house in Portman Square. The lease of the house in Suffolk – Brockley Hall – which had belonged to Robert Brendon had come to an end, and Joan had no wish to let it again. She was tired of London, and Glencairn thought it a good idea she should live there as much as she liked, and have the amusement of doing up the house. It was a comfortable Georgian house, not large, with a wide kitchen garden. Joan stayed there a great deal, and asked her uncle and aunt and other friends to visit her, but she came up to London when Glencairn wanted her. She stayed in the country three weeks at Whitsuntide, and then came to London in June, when Glencairn wished to entertain.

It had been announced in the newspapers that Dorzan was going to give a short farewell season in London. When Joan saw the announcement she talked about it to her husband in the most natural manner in the world and said she hoped he would see her as much as he liked. Not long after her season had begun Glencairn and Joan were invited to a supper party given by Harold Glaisher, who owned one of the large Conservative newspapers, the *Daily Record*. Harold Glaisher was fond of artists and of French acting, and among the guests were Alfredo Chiaromonte and his famous wife. The supper indeed was given for them. Glencairn sat on one side of Dorzan at supper and Joan was next to Chiaromonte. She found him charming. He told her this was Dorzan's positively last farewell to the stage. She found acting too exhausting; they were both fond of the country, and he had a villa on Lake Garda. Joan and Alfredo talked Italian together, and they had many friends in common. He said, among other things, that he wanted to go to Scotland – he was fond of shooting – as his wife had never been to Scotland and was longing to see it.

'You must certainly come to Travistacore,' said Joan.

And that same evening she met a Florence acquaintance, Theodore Walton, the painter. He reminded her of what he called her promise to let him paint her portrait, although Joan was not conscious of having made any promise. Walton approached

Glencairn, who was delighted with the idea, and arrangements were made then and there for her to sit to him.

When Joan and her husband were driving back from the party, Joan said to her husband:

'The Chiaromontes are thinking of going to Scotland. I told him that they must of course come and stay with us.'

'Yes, we might ask them,' said Glencairn, to whom the same idea had occurred, though he had not liked to express it.

Glencairn went to the French play nearly every night, and Joan sometimes went with him. She was able to see Dorzan act in the plays which had been forbidden before, such as *Frou-Frou* and *La Femme de Claude* and *Une Visite de Noces*, and she was swept away by Dorzan's genius and her nervous force, her charm and the almost intolerable poignancy of her pathos.

Joan did not meet the Chiaromontes again, but the day before the French season ended Glencairn said to Joan at breakfast:

'I have asked the Chiaromontes to Glencairn for the 12th. We will send the *Firefly* for them. He will do very well – he's an excellent shot. Neufchateau is coming.'

'And his wife?'

'No, she can't come. I don't see her on the hills somehow,' said Glencairn. He chuckled. 'By the way, how is the portrait getting on?'

'Very well,' said Joan; 'it's nearly finished.'

Just before the Glencairns left London, Joan received a civil letter from Dorzan saying she was bitterly disappointed but that she would not be able to come to Scotland after all. She was obliged to stay in France to wind up several matters of business connected with her theatrical career, but her husband would be delighted to avail himself of Lord Glencairn's hospitality.

When Joan heard this news she resolved that she would not be the only woman in this shooting party, but that she would go to Brockley. She told Glencairn at once, and he seemed to think this quite a good idea.

'You can come to Travistacore later,' he said, 'and ask anyone you like.'

Joan went to Brockley towards the end of July, and the Cantillons stayed with her for a week, but they left her before the 12th of August, as they too were going to Scotland for the shooting.

Joan got a brief note from Glencairn telling her that his guests had arrived, and that the prospects for the 12th were promising. Then she heard no more. It was three days after the 12th, a gorgeous sleepy August afternoon. Joan had been giving a small croquet party, to which she had asked the vicar and his wife, and one or two neighbours. They had played croquet all the afternoon and had had tea in the garden, and now they had gone away and Joan was walking round the garden by herself when the footman brought her a telegram.

'Wait a minute,' she said, 'there may be an answer.'

She felt instinctively that it was bad news. It was from Glencairn. It read as follows: 'Fatal accident out shooting today; Chiaromonte killed. Shall come south as soon as possible. Writing London.'

'There is an answer,' she said, and she walked into the house. She telegraphed to her husband that she would meet him in London when he wished. In the meantime she decided to wait till she heard from him.

The news was in the next morning's *Times*.

Count Chiaromonte, the husband of the famous actress, Mademoiselle Anaïs Dorzan, had been accidentally shot while walking-up grouse on the moors of Travistacore, the seat of the Earl of Glencairn. But this was not all. The man who had fired the shot which had killed Count Chiaromonte was the Earl of Glencairn himself.

Later on in the morning Joan had another telegram from her husband saying that he was in bed and crippled with lumbago, and unable to come to London. Joan decided to go to Scotland and telegraphed that she would do so. She went up to London and found a letter from Glencairn. He told her briefly how the accident had happened. They were walking in line – Neufchateau was on the extreme left, then Chiaromonte, then himself and Dr Maclean. Chiaromonte had got too far ahead; some birds got up, and at that moment Chiaromonte had stooped to pick up a dead bird. He could not be seen either by Glencairn or Maclean. Glencairn had fired both barrels and shot him. Maclean did everything that was possible, but there was nothing to be done. Glencairn said that he and Neufchateau were coming to London the next day. This was before his plans were changed.

Joan went north by the night train. She found Glencairn in bed. The day of the accident, almost immediately after it had happened, it had begun to rain and had rained hard. Glencairn had been drenched to the skin, and the next morning when he woke he realized that, so far from being able to travel, he couldn't move. Neufchateau undertook to do all that was necessary. He was going to Paris with the body. Chiaromonte had left instructions that he was to be buried in Paris. His wife had telegraphed from Paris to Glencairn.

Joan heard all this from her husband. He didn't refer to the accident. She then went to have her bath and breakfast, saying she would come back to him later. Just as she was finishing breakfast Dr Maclean arrived, and as soon as he had seen his patient Joan had a long talk with him alone. He said that Glencairn must stay in bed for the present. There was no question of his getting up. He was not happy about him. It was not only lumbago. He had caught a chill and he had a temperature, which showed no signs of going down. The doctor then told Joan the story of the accident in detail.

'It was certainly the poor man's fault,' he ended up.

'You think so, really?' said Joan.

'I do. His lordship was in no way to blame.'

'I'm glad you think that.'

'I do think it. I'm sure of it.'

'There aren't inquests, are there, in Scotland, but is there anything else? Something to do with the Fiscal? Didn't he have to do anything...?'

'No,' said Maclean. 'I was present. I saw the accident happen and I wrote the certificate. Nothing else was necessary. It was an accident such as will only happen once in a million times,' he said.

When this conversation came to an end Joan had a feeling of immense relief, as if a huge weight had been lifted from her; but she did not face the fact; she was frightened by the thought and would not admit it.

As soon as Maclean left the house, Joan went back to her husband and sat by his bed.

'You know exactly what happened,' said

Glencairn. 'I needn't tell you the whole story again.'

'Oh no,' she said hurriedly, 'I quite understand what happened. What about Chiaromonte's relations?'

'He's got no near relations alive, except one sister who married an American. I don't know where she is. His mother, who was very old, died about two years ago. He had no property in Italy, Neufchateau said, and no possessions except his villa on one of the lakes and a little house at Neuilly in Paris.'

'I suppose he will leave that to her.'

'I suppose so. Neufchateau has behaved nobly.'

'They were great friends, weren't they?'

'Yes. They had known each other for years. Chiaromonte had lived a great deal in Paris. What did Maclean tell you?' Glencairn asked, after a pause.

'About what?'

'About the accident.'

'He said it was the most extraordinary piece of bad luck; a thing that could only happen once in a million times.'

'Did he say I oughtn't to have fired?'

'No.'

'He should have.'

'He said it was impossible to see Chiaromonte. If anyone could have seen him, he would.'

'Maclean isn't very keen-sighted.'

125

'Yes, but he always wears spectacles. He said that the tweed Chiaromonte was wearing was indistinguishable from the heather; like the protective plumage of a bird.'

'Except that it wasn't protective in his case. It was lucky Maclean was there, wasn't it?'

'But he was too late to do anything.'

'For Chiaromonte, yes – but for me...'

'What do you mean?'

'I mean he was able to write the certificate; to certify that it was an accident.'

'You mean there might have been an... But I thought there were no inquests in Scotland?'

'There's the Fiscal.'

'But even then–'

'You mean Maclean would have given the certificate anyhow.'

'I hope so.'

'I wonder.'

'What do you mean?'

'I believe he *would* have written it anyhow.'

'Of course.'

'Why of course?'

'What else could he do?'

'Nothing, if he thought it *was* an accident.'

'You mean you think he might have thought...?'

'Yes.'

'But he couldn't have.'

'You think that would have been impossible.'

'Yes, of course – impossible.'

'Nobody, you think, could have thought it wasn't an accident?'

'Nobody.'

'You never thought so – for a moment?'

'Of course not; not for a moment.'

'And if – supposing–'

'What?'

'Supposing it hadn't been–'

'Don't let's talk any more about it.'

'No, we must. I don't believe you never thought that, Joan.'

'I thought nothing.'

'Didn't you, Joan?'

'Nothing.'

'You guessed nothing?'

'I don't know what you mean.'

'Don't you, Joan? I think you do. I think you always knew, but if you didn't you must know now, and I must tell you even if you know already. It wasn't an accident, Joan. You knew *that*.'

Joan said nothing. Her face seemed frozen into an unearthly calm, but her eyes spoke. She gave her husband a long look of serious, deep-reaching, all-embracing sympathy, mingled with an immense sadness, beyond all words and all means and modes of expression, that pierced him to the core of his being. He went on talking calmly and steadily as if he were discussing the most ordinary fact.

'But I don't know if you knew this,' he went on. 'It wasn't in the least premeditated, and it was done on the spur of the moment. I didn't see him when I shot, but I knew he was there. I had seen him a moment before. Maclean didn't see him – I knew that. I knew I was safe. It was a sudden irresistible temptation, and I gave in to it at once. I said to myself, 'I think I will kill Alfredo Chiaromonte,' and I did. Of course the moment it was done I knew it was useless and silly; that it affected nothing either in the present or the future, and left the past as it was. I have done for him, for her, for myself, and worst of all, for you.'

Joan said nothing, but bent over him and took his hand and pressed it.

'I was right, then. You did know,' he said.

'It's time you had a sleep,' said Joan. 'I will give you your medicine.'

She thought he was looking flushed, and his hand was that of a feverish man.

She gave him his medicine and said:

'I will leave you to have a sleep now, and come back later.'

She went downstairs into the library, which looked upon the sea, and thought how strange life was. What had happened had brought her and her husband together for the first time as never before, and as nothing else could have done, in a strange, mysterious and tragic manner.

'But the tragedy isn't over,' Joan said to herself. 'It's only just begun.'

The next three days passed uneventfully. Glencairn's condition remained about the same. He would be feverish in the evening, spend a restless night, and be better in the morning. Dr Maclean came every morning. He said there was nothing to be anxious about. All Glencairn needed was warmth and bed. He would be all right in a few days. His lumbago was better and he would move about with comfort.

A letter came from Paris from Neufchateau giving an account of Chiaromonte's funeral. Dorzan had been there, but none of Chiaromonte's relations, and the day after the funeral she had entered a convent.

Joan spent most of her time by Glencairn's bedside, reading aloud to him: the sporting news from *The Times,* or a novel. He had been in bed nearly a week when Dr Maclean told him that he might get up the next day. His lungs were clear and his temperature satisfactory, although it still went up a little at night.

Glencairn's bedroom, which was on the first floor, opened on a long gallery, at the end of which there was a large window going down to the floor and opening on a stone balcony, with a hard stone terrace about forty feet below.

Early on Sunday morning the servants

found Glencairn's body on the terrace. He had opened the window in his sleep and walked over the balcony into space and fallen on the flagstones. He had on a dressing-gown and was carrying a bedroom candle, which was found near the body. For the second time in a fortnight Dr Maclean had to sign a certificate of accidental death, and the prophecy of the gypsy came true in the case of Ian Glencairn.

CHAPTER 10

Robert Keith was the last survivor of one of the oldest of the old English Catholic families. He had not been in England for ten years. He had just come back from India and was enjoying his first days in London. He felt a stranger in a strange world. He had been to his club and met a few acquaintances there who did not appear to be aware that he had been absent longer than a week, or farther than Newmarket, and seemed to him to talk a strange language. At last he ran across a friend, Charles Baillie, Captain RN, he had known as a boy at school, and who had passed into the *Britannia* when he had gone to the Oratory at Birmingham. Their paths had crossed since several times, although they had seldom seen much of each other. When Baillle had been stationed at Portsmouth, and Keith's home was not far off, Baillie, who was a Catholic, had married Keith's sister Margaret, and later, when Keith went on active service with his regiment, they had met in China. Later Keith had gone to India, whence he had just returned. His parents were, both of them, dead. His only brother, who had inherited the family house in Hampshire, had been the victim of a series of misfortunes. His young wife had died in childbirth; the baby had died as well. He had had financial troubles and had been forced to mortgage his estate and then to sell the house, which was historically interesting and beautiful within and without, to a rich heiress. He had migrated to London, and died there shortly afterwards, childless and alone, and comparatively young, leaving the little that remained to him to his younger brother. The death of Robert's brother was followed almost immediately by that of an aunt, the wife of his mother's brother, and this death changed the course not only of his life but of those of his sister and his brother-in-law. His aunt, Lady Ursula Keith, was a widow; her children were all dead. She had nearer relations than Margaret and Robert Keith – her brother's children – but she had quarrelled with her brother over his marriage and had never spoken to his wife. She was fond of her niece, Margaret; she approved of Charles Baillie, and realized that their circumstances were difficult. So when she died she left a house and a small estate in Scotland, called Ardveg, to Margaret Baillie, and to Robert enough money to enable him to leave the Army and to settle in England for good, which he had wished but had never been able to do. He was tired of India, tired of the

East, tired of the Army, and he longed, so he thought, for England and country life. And now, he thought to himself, he could marry if he wished to. It was surely not too late. He was only thirty-six, and although he had been tanned and aged by the Orient and his hair was thin, his activity was undiminished. He was a lonely man, but he longed to escape from a position in which he felt himself buried. He was a finely built man, square and clean-looking, with straight features and melancholy eyes like those of a bloodhound. When people saw him they would say, 'What an interesting face, he must be interesting to talk to'; but in conversation Robert Keith was strangely uncommunicative, and you had to know him extremely well before he would talk except in monosyllables. People wondered why he had never married. There had indeed been one romance: a girl he had fallen in love with when he was a subaltern, just before he went out to India; but her parents had been against it; he had nothing to offer; she had little to bring, and there was the difference of religion, and ultimately she married Bernard Stillman, who was in the City and later on became a baronet and a Member of Parliament, one of the pillars of the Whig Party and an extremely rich man, which was thought most satisfactory. His brother-in-law, Charles, had done well in the Navy and had been promoted rapidly, but he too had longed for some time in vain for country life. He had a large family, and he and Margaret had lived all over the place until the unexpected legacy had changed matters. Charles Baillie was as fine looking a man as his brother-in-law, but in every way a contrast; his features were sharp and his eyes piercing; he was high-spirited and talkative, and expressed himself with an untaught felicity and distinction.

'I only arrived yesterday,' Robert was saying. They were standing in the morning room of the club and partaking of a glass of port and a biscuit.

'What treat would you like for your first day?' asked Charles.

'I should like to go to the Academy,' said Robert, 'and then luncheon, and then to Lord's to look at the cricket. I should like to dine at some cheerful place, and go to the play.'

'Well, I'm at your service till tomorrow night, when I go north. You shall come with me to Ardveg; I am going to telegraph to Margaret at once.'

They then strolled up St James's Street to Burlington House. It was a hot morning in July; London was becoming empty, but the Academy was crowded. The most popular pictures that year were by Millais (*The Beefeater*) and Leighton (*The Music Lesson*); and there was a crowd round Frith's *Nothing ven-*

ture, nothing win. Robert and Charles walked through the rooms, Charles voluble and explanatory and Robert silent, and Robert took more interest in the spectators than in the pictures on the walls. He was arrested by one picture which hung on the line in one of the smaller rooms. It was called, *Portrait of the Countess of Glencairn*, by Theodore Walton. It was a portrait in profile. The sitter was looking straight in front of her, her hair coiled on the top of her head in the fashion of the day. She was dressed in black with high tight sleeves that reached to the wrist, and a necktie tied in a bow. Her complexion was like ivory; the features straight and well cut; but what was remarkable about the picture was the expression of gravity and serenity and yet of sadness in the face. The expression seemed much too old for her age. Robert Keith stood in front of the picture and said nothing for a long time.

'It's by Walton,' said Charles. 'They say he is the coming man and that he'll be President of the Academy some day. He's never done anything better than this. It's exactly like her. She lives not far from us in Scotland. Poor woman, she's had a bad time. She lived abroad all her life in Italy as a girl, and she had only just come to England and married when her husband killed a fellow by accident out shooting, and a week later he fell out of a window walking in his sleep and was killed.'

'And now she lives in Scotland?'

'Yes, Glencairn left her Killeen, a small shooting-lodge. She had a house in Suffolk but she's let it. The castle and estate went with the title to a distant cousin. Glencairn left nothing else except a London house, which has been sold. He was badly off – a spendthrift – and they say he only married her for her money, and then spent it all, but I don't believe that's true; firstly because she hadn't got much; secondly because she was just the sort of out-of-the-way person who would be likely to attract a man like Glencairn.'

'What was he like?'

'Oh, a traveller, a rolling stone, and a rake – cosmopolitan and knowledgeable about all sorts of different things – good company.'

'I suppose he was older than she was?'

'Yes, a good deal.'

'She must be a charming woman to look at if she is anything like that.'

'She is like that, and she is uncommon, but you shall see her for yourself. She lives close to us, and we'll get Margaret to ask her over. She doesn't go out; she sees nobody except Margaret, and we'll get her to come over to luncheon or something while you're there.'

'It certainly is an attractive picture,' said Robert, and he went on looking at it.

The next evening Robert Keith travelled north to stay with the Baillies at Ardveg. He was given a warm welcome by his sister and the children. There were two boys and four girls. The two elder girls were grown up; the boys at school. Margaret Baillie had once been beautiful and was still good-looking: she looked tired and worn-out, and indeed she was. She had not enough energy to live up to her husband's high spirits. She had found life a struggle. Her husband had had little beyond his pay; she had had nothing. She had followed him to Malta and Gibraltar, and various ports. Then there had been the bringing-up of the children; school for the boys; but just when Charles had been promoted to captain, the death of the aunt and the unexpected legacy to Margaret had changed her fortune, brought her relief, and enabled her husband to fulfil his dream of retiring from the Navy and living a country life. As far as she was concerned this windfall had come too late; she was worn-out by child-bearing, unselfishness, piety and the struggle to make both ends meet, and the noise of children in overcrowded houses. The windfall which had changed the life of Robert Keith and the Baillies had happened just after Lord Glencairn's death.

The day after Robert arrived he asked his sister whether she knew any of her neighbours.

'Charles has made friends with some of them,' she said. 'He shoots at Laracor with young De Felton, Lady De Felton's son, and there are others.'

'Charles told me of a Lady Glencairn,' said Robert.

'Yes, she lives not far off at Killeen. It's only three miles off. I know her, but she doesn't go out. Why?'

'We saw her picture in the Academy, that's all.'

Charles came up at that moment and caught on to the conversation.

'Robert was smitten by the lady's portrait,' he said. 'He must see the original.'

'If we see her at Mass on Sunday I will ask her to luncheon,' said Margaret, 'but she's not often there.'

On Sundays the Baillies drove to their parish church, which was in the village of Strathmorn. On the Sunday after their arrival they did not meet Lady Glencairn, but on the following Sunday, just before the 12th, she was there, and Margaret Baillie stopped and talked to her afterwards and asked her if she would come over to luncheon. She was sorry; this was impossible; she had her uncle and aunt and their children staying with her; but wouldn't the Baillies come over to tea, and wouldn't Mrs Baillie bring her brother. Margaret had taken the opportunity of introducing Robert to Lady Glencairn.

They were shooting all the week. They went over to tea the following Sunday and found the Cantillons there, and Margaret asked the whole party to dinner, and they came on the following Wednesday, and Robert Keith sat next to Joan. She came up to the expectations that had been raised in his heart by the picture. He thought he had never met so attractive a woman in his life. She was dressed in the deep mourning which showed off the extreme whiteness of her skin, the classic quality of her features. Her face looked as if it had been carved in marble. Never, thought Robert, had he seen a calmer face; but her eyes made you forget all the rest. They were still more striking, he thought, than in the picture. They were so sad; so serious; so full of precocious wisdom; for she was absurdly young to have such sad eyes; but then, of course, she had been through a great deal. They did not talk to each other much at dinner. She asked him about India; Robert was even more silent than she was; but Charles Baillie, who was sitting next to Mrs Cantillon, embraced the whole table with his talk, and drowned the conversation in loud and boisterous anecdotes. After dinner they had music; Margaret Baillie sang some songs in Italian from *Lucrezia Borgia* and the *Barbiere*. She had a crystal voice, but she was not a good musician.

'Do you like music?' Robert Keith asked Lady Glencairn.

'No, I'm afraid I don't,' said Joan, who was suffering from Margaret's British way of pronouncing Italian. 'I am afraid I have no ear.'

'No more have I.'

They were both relieved when Charles Baillie advanced to the piano and sang 'Drink, puppy, drink'. There was nothing to find fault with in his accent or intonation, and they begged him to sing something else, which he did with alacrity.

When Joan and the Cantillons drove home, Mrs Cantillon asked her what she thought of Robert Keith.

'He is silent,' said Joan, 'and shy, but he is the kind of man I like. I feel *certain* about him, just as one does about certain kinds of dogs.'

'Yes, he's a gentlemanlike fellow,' said Horace Cantillon.

The following Sunday Robert Keith walked over to pay his respects, and he stayed to tea.

CHAPTER 11

When the tragedy of Travistacore and Chiaromonte's death culminated in the further climax of Glencairn's sudden and tragic end, Joan neither turned her face to the wall to say, 'My life is over,' nor did she look forward with exultation into the future and say, 'My life is now going to begin.'

Life had crashed about her like a huge temple overthrown by an earthquake; but after the shock had subsided she was conscious among the ruins and the desolation that she must not sit and mope, but build herself a hut. She knew that certain irreparable things had happened; that her soul had been scarred and seared in a particular way by Destiny, but she felt certain that this was not the end; that there were many other things in store for her; that though a vital branch had been lopped from her, others went on sprouting, and who knows, there might even be a certain amount of happiness in store for her. When she accepted Glencairn she had been attracted by him, she was ready to love him; and then had come the first crisis, ending in their virtual separation; but Joan had always felt that, in spite of everything, all might come well some day, that deep down in his heart Glencairn was capable of loving her, if once he could come-to from the intoxication of his passion for Dorzan. She had felt he understood her and that she had understood him. Then, after the Chiaromonte tragedy, she had been certain of this; and then the end had come. After her husband's death she set herself to face the trivial duties and business of her daily life, and she lived from day to day. She lived alone, morally, that is to say. She saw quite a number of people, but there was no one in whom she could confide. Her father had been her only friend, and since his death she had not made another. She was fond of her uncle and aunt, but never in the least tempted to confide in either of them. She might possibly have opened her heart to Agatha had Agatha been in England, but she was in India. Joan was not a woman who felt an urgent need to confide in anyone, least of all in another woman. She found plenty to do and plenty of things to keep herself busy with. She was fond of her surroundings, fond of the people; she was an expert fisherwoman and threw a beautiful line; she was a good water-colourist; she understood building, architecture and carpentering; she was a practical gardener. She was busy; occupied all day; and she found by the evening that she was too sleepy for reading. She had ceased to take any interest in books when her father died. He was the only person with whom she cared to discuss old books, and as for modern literature, she had not discovered it. She had no one to discover it with. She preferred living in Scotland to Suffolk. In Suffolk there were too many neighbours, and she was independent in Scotland, and could breathe freely. Her villa at Florence was still let. She had no house in London. Lord Glencairn's house had been sold by the trustees; she had no wish to live in London. She was contented where she was. She had enough to live on, but it was true that Glencairn had managed in one year to make a large hole in her fortune. She sometimes saw her neighbours; but these lived, all of them, at a considerable distance from Killeen, and as most of them were busy shooting and fishing during the week, and did not care to make long expeditions on Sunday, it was not often that she met them.

The Baillies were the only neighbours she saw at all regularly. She liked Captain Baillie and she admired his wife, but she felt oppressed by her. Although Joan had lived all her life in a Catholic country and had been brought up by an Irish Catholic nurse, who was still with her, Joan had never come across practical Catholic piety. The Italians she had known had taken their religion as a matter of course – the men with a light and polite scepticism, the women with practical respect. The Church for them was a matter of a certain seasonal ritual, and marriages and funerals. It did not seem to enter into their daily life or to affect it. With Margaret Baillie it was a different matter; her religion seemed to be to her all-important; not that she appeared to be bigoted or narrow-minded; she was the soul of charity, and not even critical. But you were conscious – you could not be unconscious – of her extra-ordinary piety. It was a thing you felt at once. It struck you like a blow. And Joan, although she admired it, felt she would find it hard to live up to. She had lived all her life among the sceptical; her father was scep-ticism incarnate. Mabel San Felice had been gaily sceptical; her husband, Glencairn, had been not only ironically sceptical but frankly cynical; and the only influence on the other side she had met with was that of Kathleen, whom she regarded as being incurably, fan-tastically superstitious. With Captain Baillie she felt no bar or barrier; he was cheerful, gay and good-humoured; but with Margaret she felt a hidden bar; she felt that Margaret felt the lack of something in her which made a bar between them. Not that she ever discussed it.

Joan went to Mass at Strathmorn village sometimes on Sundays – to please Kathleen more than anything else. She had no religious faith, and she knew little of the theory or practice of the Catholic religion, and that little she had gleaned from Kathleen; but she respected the religion of other people; she was fond of ritual, custom and tradition; she felt an innate revolt against dogmatic unbelief. Her father had taught her to disbelieve in disbelief which, he used to say, was as shallow as any of the creeds.

And now there was a new figure on the stage – Robert Keith. He seemed to be remarkably like his sister Margaret, only lower in tone, more reserved, more silent. Joan liked him, but she suspected that his moral and intellectual outlook was probably the same as that of his sister, yet with him she was so far unconscious of any barrier; she felt comfortable in his presence.

The Cantillons and their children stayed with her during the whole month of August. Her Uncle Horace was a keen fisherman and there was good fishing at Killeen, and the Baillies asked him to shoot with them.

Mrs Cantillon hoped beyond all things that Joan would marry again, and when Robert Keith's visits began to grow frequent she wondered whether perhaps the right person had not arrived on the scene.

Robert Keith stayed with his sister the whole of August and September. He was a frequent visitor at Killeen. He would stroll over on Sunday afternoons or sometimes late in the afternoon on weekdays and stay for a long time, not saying much: discussing the garden and local affairs. One day Joan asked him what were his plans for the future. He said he wanted to settle down in the country.

'I am sick to death of foreign parts,' he said. 'I've had enough of the East. I *should* have liked Suffolk,' he said, 'only...'

'Only what?'

'I don't know of any place there which would do for me.'

'My house will be to let soon,' said Joan. 'I have decided not to go back there. I like living here best.'

'The only reason I wanted to live in Suffolk,' said Robert, 'was that I thought you might be living there too.'

Joan was pulling up weeds as they were talking. It was a lovely clear September evening. She was talking in that semi-absent-minded, semi-preoccupied tone which people use when they are doing something else while they are talking.

'You will soon make friends,' she said; 'there are a great many people there, if anything too many people.'

'You don't understand,' he said. 'I don't want people.'

'But you needn't really see much of them; I didn't. I was really a bad neighbour.'

'You don't understand,' he said again.

'There is only one person I want to see.'

Joan was so startled that she stopped weeding and looked up.

'Don't you understand now?' he said. 'Haven't you always understood? There is only one person I want – and want for always.'

Joan was dumbstruck with astonishment. It had never occurred to her that Robert Keith could possibly feel or say such things. There was no reason why it should not have occurred to her; but it had not. Her Aunt Amy had seen the possibility at once, but had wisely said nothing. Joan for some reason or other had thought, both that it was out of the question anyone should want to marry her, and that it was out of the question that Robert Keith should want to marry at all. Both suppositions were entirely baseless.

Joan had turned pink with surprise and she felt her ears were burning; she did not know what to say.

'Oh, don't say anything more, Colonel Keith,' she said. 'I couldn't marry anyone.'

'We will say no more about it,' said Keith, and he went on talking of ordinary things as though the incident had not happened.

But when he left, Joan was still trembling with excitement and said to herself: 'Is it true I couldn't marry anyone? Could I marry Robert Keith?' She was not, she

147

knew, in love with him, but she might love him. She liked him immensely. Then she knew she was comparing him with Alexander, and it was the thought of Alexander that was the real obstacle.

Robert Keith went south at the end of October, but he came back to Ardveg at Christmas-time. Life went on normally, just as before. Robert often saw Joan, but he never referred to his declaration, or even said anything remotely of the same nature again. In the spring Joan went south and stayed with her uncle and aunt at Littlewood, and at Easter she went to Florence and spent a month with the San Felices. On her return home she went to Scotland and stayed there all the summer. Her aunt and uncle came to her in August with the children, and later Countess San Felice and her daughter Angelica. In August, Robert Keith was once more with the Baillies, and life was going on in exactly the same way as usual.

The Baillies made the acquaintance of the San Felices and asked them to dinner. When they got home, Countess San Felice sat in Joan's bedroom while she undressed and brushed her hair.

'What did you think of them, Aunt Mabel?' Joan asked.

'Mrs Baillie is a saint,' she said, 'Captain Baillie is a dear, and the other one – Keith – is one in a thousand. He does not say much, but he is so – so *right.*'

She had sat next to him at dinner.

'He is absent-minded, my dear, when you are there.'

'What do you mean?'

'He is in love with you.'

'Oh, nonsense, Aunt Mabel.'

'Dearest Joan, what I have always liked about you is your sense, your honesty and your frankness. You are not going to be foolish now, are you? You must know he loves you.'

'He asked me to marry him last year.'

'And what?'

'I told him I would never marry.'

'That isn't true, is it?'

'I don't know; perhaps not. I like him. I like him very much. I thought he had got over it. I don't think I should be the right wife for him. And then I don't think I could marry again, unless I felt sure – unless I felt I couldn't help it – and I don't feel that. I can very well help marrying Robert Keith.'

Countess San Felice understood that Joan was thinking of her first marriage. She knew no details; nothing of what had happened; but she divined there must have been great disillusion if not drama. All she said was:

'Would you like him to marry someone else?'

'I should be disappointed; I should mind a little.'

'I understand what you mean, but I believe that marriages which are made when people can help it are happier than those which are made when people can't help it. My marriage with Carlo was arranged by our parents: we were not forced into it, but we were not in love with one another; and nothing could have turned out better. I miss Carlo every day. I believe you would be perfectly happy married to Keith. It is ridiculous to think you can spend the whole of the rest of your life alone.'

'Perhaps he won't ask me.'

'I think he is a quiet but determined man, and the kind of man who gets what he wants in the long run, however long he has to wait for it.'

'When he proposed last year I thought it out of the question, but now I think differently. But oh, Aunt Mabel, is it wise? It's such a lottery! such a risk! I am, after all, happy as I am.'

'You are meant for other things – you are meant for married life and to have children.'

'I'm not an old maid, Aunt Mabel, I'm a widow. And then Robert Keith is so silent, isn't he?'

'That is what I like. I feel sure about him.'

'I feel all that,' said Joan, 'but is it enough?'

'That is the essential. The other things don't matter; one finds them elsewhere.'

'I wonder.'

Joan was a long time getting to sleep that night. She lay awake and thought and thought. Her father would have liked Robert Keith; of that she felt certain. He would probably have refused to give any advice.

'But perhaps,' she thought to herself, 'he is not thinking of asking me.'

He was. He was thinking of nothing else. A few days later he came to fish in the river. The Cantillons and the San Felices were still there, but the Countess had skilfully asked that she and the others might go and shop in the village while Joan fished in the river. So Joan and Robert Keith fished in the river together. They walked home together to tea, and he asked her to marry him. This time Joan accepted him.

CHAPTER 12

They were married in December quietly in London and they went abroad for their honeymoon to Rome and to Florence. They came back to England in May.

They stayed for a time at Littlewood with the Cantillons, and then they went to Scotland. Joan was expecting a baby, and her aunt and uncle were coming to stay at Killeen so as to be with her. Joan was happy; happy with her husband. She loved him: he loved her. She considered herself to be perfectly happy. Robert was not only a good husband, but he had not turned into somebody different and unexpected. It was the end of August. It was hot. Joan was feeling desperately ill. She was sitting one morning in the small drawing-room writing letters while her aunt wrote at another table, when the servant brought in a telegram for Mrs Cantillon.

Mrs Cantillon opened it, read it, and said nothing. Joan, who was not looking at her, knew at once it had brought bad news.

'Thank you,' said Mrs Cantillon to the butler, 'there's no answer.'

The butler left the room and Mrs Cantillon sat still with the telegram in her hand. Joan got up.

'Aunt Amy,' she said, 'what is it?'

She clasped her aunt in her arms and Mrs Cantillon cried and cried, her body shaking with silent sobs.

She gave Joan the telegram.

'It's Agatha,' she said.

The telegram said that Agatha had died as the result of an accident. It was from Alexander, and he was starting home directly.

'What will Horace do?' said Mrs Cantillon. 'It will break his heart.'

He was out shooting with Robert and his boys. He was told in the afternoon when he came back, and his grief was piteous to witness. Mrs Cantillon was calm and said they must do everything to prevent Joan from being upset at such a moment.

Two days later Joan began to feel worse, and they sent for Dr Maclean, whom Joan trusted more than any doctor in the world.

Twelve hours later a fine boy was easily born. He was baptized Andrew. Joan drifted after her hours of pain on an ocean of helpless content.

But one thought was worrying her throughout everything: when would Alexander arrive? And would he come to Scotland? She passionately wished him not to come, but felt she could not say so. But the matter settled itself. Alexander Luttrell had intended to leave India immediately after sending his cable. He was expected to arrive in three weeks from that date, but it so happened that he was delayed. Joan was up and about in three weeks' time after the baby was born, and the Cantillons left her and went south to London. Alexander Luttrell arrived about a fortnight later. He saw the Cantillons in London and then he went to stay with his mother in the country. He decided to leave the Army and go in for politics. Agatha's death had been due to a miscarriage brought on by a fall. Joan heard all this from her aunt.

She and Robert stayed in Scotland the whole winter till the next June. Joan was perfectly contented; her baby was a joy to her. But she gradually noticed that Robert was not contented. In theory he had been longing all his life to come home to the country, and especially a wild part of the country like Scotland. But in practice the East had bitten him too deeply, had infected him too strongly with its microbe for him ever to get over it. The winter in the North seemed to him intolerably dark. He longed once more for sunshine and light and warmth. It affected him physically. He started a permanent cough, and Dr Maclean told Joan that he must not spend another winter in the North. Then there was the question, where were they to go? Robert did not like Florence or

Rome, not to live in, that is to say; he did not care for foreign society. He missed the Indian life. He missed polo and the club. He was profoundly insular. It was Charles Baillie who settled the matter for them. He was going out next winter to Malta to stay at Admiralty House with the Commander-in-Chief of the Mediterranean Fleet, who was a great friend of his. Why should not Joan and Robert come out to Malta and take a house there? The climate was warm; living was cheap; Robert would meet some old friends and he would enjoy the life there.

Joan thought this would be an excellent idea. The Cantillons had asked them to stay at Littlewood for Whitsuntide, and Joan, although she was reluctant to do so, as she feared she would meet Alexander there, could think of no reason for refusing, especially as Robert enjoyed the society of Horace Cantillon; also because he wished to go south for a time.

They went down to Littlewood on the Saturday. Before they started, Joan learnt that her fears were well-grounded, because her aunt wrote to her and told her that she had asked Alexander Luttrell to meet her, as well as the Faussets and Alexander's sister, Lady Alice Haslewood, and her husband, Cuthbert Haslewood.

Joan and Robert arrived late. Joan had arranged this on purpose so that after being welcomed by her aunt they could go and dress for dinner at once without seeing any of the other guests.

They came down punctually in time for dinner, and Joan found Mrs Fausset full of bustling voluble egoism, arguing with Mrs Cantillon as to the placing of the guests. The next arrivals were Lady Alice and her husband, who was said to be doing very well in parliament, but was handicapped by a slight and occasional stammer. Alexander was the last to arrive. 'He always was unpunctual,' said Joan to herself. 'How fortunate,' she thought, 'things have turned out as they have. As it is, I shall no more mind seeing him *now* than if he were a complete stranger.' Just as she was thinking that, he came into the room and walked straight up to Joan and said: 'Will you introduce me to your husband,' which Joan did.

Then Mrs Cantillon asked him to take Joan in to dinner. They went into the long oak-panelled dining-room. There was a round table, and Joan was sitting between Alexander and Cuthbert Haslewood. Her husband was on the other side of the table, on Mrs Cantillon's right. It was for Joan an uncanny experience. She felt as if she had turned to ice, or rather as if she were not alive; as if nothing was real and she was living in a dream, when one accepts the intrusion of the dead although one sometimes knows they couldn't be there. And the terrible thing was that although she kept on saying to herself, while she pretended to listen to Cuthbert Haslewood's denunciation of Mr Gladstone, 'He is no more to me now than a complete stranger,' she knew this was not true. There came a moment three-quarters of the way through dinner, the moment she had done her best to postpone as long as possible, when she was obliged to turn and talk to Alexander, as Cuthbert Haslewood had begun to talk to her aunt, and Alexander's neighbour's attention had also been claimed. She said something about the tulips on the table.

'They remind one,' he said, 'of Florence.'

'Yes, they do,' she said, feeling a stab at the word Florence, and as if all that had happened at Florence belonged to another existence.

'Have you still got your villa there?' he asked.

'No,' she said. 'First I let it, and then I sold it. It is too cold for Robert. The winds are too cold in the winter and even in the spring, and the doctors say that Robert must spend the winter in a warm place, so this year we are going to Malta. Do you know Malta?'

'Yes, we stayed there on our way out. Agatha loved it. But I don't know what it would be like to live in. Do you mean to

158

settle there for good?'

'Yes, for the winters. We shall come to England for the summer or the autumn. I hear you are standing for parliament,' said Joan, and they discussed his constituency and his prospects, and once more they fell into an easy intimacy, each guessing what the other was thinking, whatever happened to be said; each being able to laugh at exactly the same kind of thing, to see things from the same angle.

'This is the first time,' thought Joan, 'I have laughed since Ian's death.' She used to laugh with Ian, but she never laughed with Robert.

Alexander was thinking the same thing. It was the first time he had laughed since he had come back from India. Dinner seemed to come to an end in a minute, and Joan was just saying, 'Oh, but I don't in the least agree,' when she was conscious that her aunt was trying to catch her eye, and that it was time for the men to be left alone. She did not have any more conversation that evening with Alexander; he played billiards with Robert; but when she went to bed her aunt came and sat with her, and asked her how she thought Alexander was.

'He looks drawn and rather white,' said Joan, 'but that, I suppose, is from living in India.'

While this conversation was going on,

Horace Cantillon, Alexander Luttrell and Robert Keith were smoking in the billiard-room and discussing politics, and Alexander was finding Robert extremely dull and difficult to elicit any response from. He wondered how and why Joan could have married so dull a man. He thought Joan had changed considerably. She had fined down in looks. She was thinner in face, and this showed off her eyes to greater advantage. She was at the same time, he thought, more mature in mind. He thought she must have gone through a great deal, and he suspected that her married life with Glencairn must have been far from easy. Altogether, the whole time he was talking politics in that billiard-room, he was thinking of Joan, and he thought of her long after he went to bed. He had been fond of Agatha: her sudden death had been an overwhelming blow; but there was no doubt that he was not only perfectly happy in Joan's company, but happier in hers than in any company. He did not compare her with the absent and find her wanting. Joan was conscious of this, and she had been determined that on no account should their intimacy be renewed, or rather resurrected. And now, to her alarm, this thing seemed to have happened in the course of one short conversation.

But once more things were settled for her. They had decided before going to Littlewood that after Whitsuntide, when the Cantillons went back to London, they would take lodgings at Brighton for a month. Robert had talked of this plan at the club in the hearing of one of his former fellow officers, a General Cray. General Cray had retired and taken a small house at Brighton, and he offered to lend it to Robert for June and July, as he and his wife wished to spend those months in London. Robert had accepted this offer, and they were to go there as soon as they left Littlewood. They had sent on the baby with the nurse and their servants. The Cantillons wanted Joan to stay on for a fortnight till they went to London. Robert said he would go on Tuesday. He thought Joan might like a little time alone with her aunt and uncle. Sunday went by quietly. They spent the day playing lawn tennis (Robert had been a good Badminton player in India). On Monday they got a telegram from the nurse at Brighton to say Andrew had a high temperature. Joan and Robert left for Brighton immediately. Mrs Cantillon begged Joan to come back as soon as she liked if she found all was well. Joan promised she would. When they arrived at Brighton they found Andrew still feverish, but when the doctor came he diagnosed the disease as being nothing more serious than chickenpox, and in three days' time he was practically well. Mrs Cantillon urged Joan by letter to come back on the following Friday or Saturday, and to bring Robert. Joan showed Robert the letter containing this proposal one morning at breakfast. Robert read it and said nothing.

'Well?' asked Joan.

'You can go, of course, if you like. I shall stay here.'

'I can't go without you,' said Joan.

'You were going to stay on at Littlewood a whole fortnight without me if Andrew hadn't been ill.'

'That was different,' she said. 'I thought Charles Baillie would be here with you.'

This was almost but not quite true. Charles Baillie, who was in London by himself and had been laid up with a cold, had thought of going to Brighton for Whitsuntide, and Robert had told him he would be there by himself on Whit Tuesday and could put him up, and he had not answered because he was still in bed: but on Saturday morning Joan met Dr Maclean in a shop. He was spending his yearly holiday in London. He said he had been to see Charles Baillie in his rooms. He was suffering from bronchitis and was being wisely kept in bed by his London doctor.

'He thinks,' said Dr Maclean, 'he is going to Brighton on Whit Tuesday to stay with the Colonel, but it will be a week before they will allow him up, or more.'

Joan, without any forethought or reason, had said nothing about this meeting to Robert. And on the Saturday she had certainly thought that she would stay a week at Littlewood, whether Charles Baillie went to Brighton or not.

'I shall certainly not leave you alone,' said Joan, 'unless Charles Baillie could come and stay next week.'

'It wouldn't be civil,' said Robert, 'to go away just as he was coming.'

'Very well,' said Joan, 'that is settled. I will write to Aunt Amy.'

Robert said nothing more to persuade her to go, and Joan had a feeling that he did not want her to go. She was at the same time both disappointed and relieved. It is all for the best, she said to herself. It is just as well that I should see no more of Alexander. Nothing good could come of it.

When Joan next heard from her aunt, Mrs Cantillon said at the end of her letter: 'If you have room it would be a kindness to ask Alexander down for a Sunday; he is so lonely.'

Joan showed the letter to Robert, who said:

'We might have asked him, but we can't now, because Charles Baillie is coming; there isn't room.'

'You never told me,' said Joan.

'I thought it was understood that he was

to come as soon as he was well enough. I told him we should expect him on Saturday unless we heard to the contrary.'

'That is the first time,' Joan said to herself, 'Robert has done anything without telling me first. There is no doubt that he does not want Alexander to come.'

Charles Baillie came at the end of the week. He stayed a few days. Then he went to London, and then north.

Two or three days later Joan heard from her aunt that Alexander had gone to his constituency.

Joan and Robert stayed at Brighton till the end of July.

Joan was still happy and perfectly contented. Her baby, Andrew, was reaching the adorable age of one. He was a strong healthy child, with large eyes. Everything, in fact, in her married life was smooth and serene. She had no quarrels with Robert, but there was one invisible barrier between them which was perhaps worse than a quarrel, and that was their religion. As has already been said, Joan's religion, although she was nominally a Catholic, had consisted of no more than an occasional going to Mass to please her nurse, Kathleen, who was still with them. She had told Robert this, knowing him to be genuinely pious, before they were married. He had laughed the matter away, since he considered that if you had been born and baptized a Catholic and married in a Catholic church all was bound to be for the best some day.

But when she had told him at the first Easter after they were married that she could not go to fulfil her Easter duties because the whole thing meant nothing to her at all, he was concerned. He suggested she should have a talk with the parish priest, Father Lang, who, besides being a scholar and a cultivated man, was exceptionally acute and sensible. This Joan flatly refused to do.

'You don't understand,' she said; 'it's not a question of this or that Church with me, or this or that dogma. I don't believe. I have got no faith. I don't believe in a future life, and I don't feel that I want to. I don't feel the existence of an all-just and all-good Providence. I should like to have faith like yours. I admire you for it; I respect you for it. I envy you. But I haven't got it, and if one hasn't got it it's no use pretending one has. I am not even a pagan. They had faith in a great deal. Perhaps you think it hypocritical of me ever to go to Mass, or to step inside a church. But I have promised Kathleen to do this. She knows I have no faith, but she prays for me to get it and she thinks that if I go to Mass I may one day be given faith. If I am, so much the better; nobody would be more pleased than I.'

When Joan said all this, Robert was

silenced. He did not attempt to argue with her. In a way it was easier for him to understand than if Joan had said she was a High Churchwoman or a Methodist. He understood Catholics, and he accepted the fact that there were many people without faith: but he did not pretend to understand the various forms of what he considered to be one great heresy.

Since Joan had lived in England she had sometimes come across Catholic converts, and she had noticed that they were different in their behaviour from her husband. He never seemed to want to parade his faith, to proselytize, or to point the moral. On the contrary, he seemed to have a kind of bitter pride in belonging to an obscure and neglected minority, as if he were a member of an old-fashioned, dignified and half-forgotten club, which was content with its obscurity, its immemorial traditions, its uncompromising rules and undeviating customs. Sometimes he would say, with an ironical smile, talking of a political appointment or job, 'So-and-so ought to get it, but they won't give it to a Catholic'; but on the whole he seldom mentioned the subject. Yet he was scrupulously punctilious in fulfilling his duties, in abstaining on Fridays and going to Mass on Sundays. When he was engaged to Joan, although she had told him what she felt, he had never really believed it.

It was not until after they had been married and after their eldest child was born that he saw it was true. Once he realized this, he accepted it and confined himself to hoping that all would come right in the end. 'The nuns,' he said, 'will pray for her.'

Joan and Robert stayed at Brighton until the end of July, when they were asked to stay for the Goodwood Races with Cuthbert Haslewood and his wife at their house in Sussex, which was not far from Arundel. This visit was to have far-reaching results on their lives. Robert was not a gambler by nature, but he was passionately fond of horses and horse-racing, and while in India he had ridden and raced a great deal. He had more or less given up riding now, after one bad fall, but he was still interested in racing. In India he had always been lucky. Indeed his good luck had been proverbial, and this was just as well, as he could in those days ill afford to lose. Since he had returned to England he had only been racing once or twice, and when he married he made a resolution to give up betting altogether. But at Goodwood he thought he would try his luck. He betted, lost, and tried to put things right by betting again, hazarding a large sum on a so-called certainty which was beaten. At the end of the meeting he found that a large hole had been made in his capital. He hoped to fill the gap at Doncaster.

Robert and Joan went to Killeen from Goodwood. Andrew and the nurse had preceded them. They had asked the Cantillons to stay with them, but they could not come till September. Mrs Cantillon asked Joan to invite Alexander Luttrell, saying that he was still so dreadfully lonely and miserable. When she showed the letter to Robert he said:

'By all means ask him on the 10th; I shan't be here, because I am going with Charles Baillie to stay with some friends of his near Doncaster.'

'Can Robert possibly be jealous of Alexander?' thought Joan. 'I don't think we'll ask him if you're not here,' she said.

'Of course you must,' said Robert. 'I shall only be away a day or two.'

Robert did go to Doncaster. Alexander was asked to Killeen, but he was prevented from coming at the last moment. And Robert, in attempting to make good his losses, lost a further considerable part of his not over-large capital.

CHAPTER 13

When Robert got back to Killeen from Doncaster he found Joan in a sad frame of mind. Kathleen, her old nurse, was desperately ill and not expected to live. The day that Robert arrived she received the Last Sacraments, and she died quietly with the coming of the dawn the next morning. Joan was at her bedside. This did not prevent Robert from breaking his disagreeable piece of news at once and from exposing the lamentable state of his affairs. Joan received the news with the utmost calm.

'We will let Killeen,' she said, 'and try and get a long lease, which I think we shall do easily, considering the shooting and the fishing, and we will stay at Malta two years on end, or longer if necessary. We shall have quite enough to live on there. The only thing which could have made that difficult was Kathleen. We couldn't have taken her, and now, sad as it is, that difficulty does not exist any longer.'

She did not add one word of reproach or blame or warning or advice. They both went to London in October, and there matters were arranged. Killeen was let for three years. Robert and Joan stayed a week at Littlewood with the Cantillons. They then started for Malta, breaking the journey at Florence, where they stayed a few days at the Villa San Felice. They arrived at Valletta at the beginning of November. They stayed at an hotel at first, until they found a house which suited them, which they were not long in doing. It was a charming little house in the Strada de Molinos. Robert began to revive as soon as he got there. It suited him. He liked the climate; he liked the people; there was a church almost at his door; he bought a polo pony; he met several old friends, and soon made many new ones. Charles Baillie, his wife and one of his daughters, came out soon after Joan and Robert, and Charles Baillie introduced them to his naval friends.

Margaret Baillie came to see Joan every day, and the more Joan saw of her the more she admired her, and the less capable she felt of imitating her example.

Joan felt that the move had been a success. The winter was gay. Joan and Robert were warmly welcomed, and they were both appreciated, although some people wondered how so seemingly vital a woman could have married so silent and quiet a man as Robert; others, how so English a man as Robert could have married someone so obviously 'foreign' as Joan. The autumn and the winter went quickly by, and in the spring Joan began to feel ill once more.

Towards the end of April, her second son was born. He was called Antony.

Joan enjoyed the summer – her first summer at Malta – a great deal more than the winter. She enjoyed the heat and the bathing and the summer life; she was sorry when it came to an end.

The second winter at Malta Joan enjoyed less. She still regretted nothing. She felt that Robert was happy; that Malta was exactly the right place for him; that they could not have chosen better, and that he liked Malta on the whole: but she could not disguise from herself the fact that she felt lonely, far more lonely in the gay and crowded life of Malta than she had felt at Killeen. She had many friends, but no friend: not one soul, man or woman, to whom she could say exactly what she felt.

But she thought to herself, 'I must get used to this. It is, after all, what happens to everyone.'

At the end of the following summer she was expecting another baby, and the Baillies came out again. A daughter was born in October. She was called Kathleen.

The Baillies stayed at Malta the whole of that winter, and at the end of the spring Joan and Robert went back with them to England.

The lease of Killeen had ended, and it was a question whether they should renew it or find a new tenant. It was no longer necessary for them to live the whole year at Malta for financial reasons. They had economized enough. They stayed a few days in London, at an hotel, and then they went north. Joan was overjoyed to get back to Scotland, but Robert, she could see, missed Malta. They stayed in Scotland, seeing a great deal of the Baillies, till the end of October. Then they went back to Malta. The question of the lease was not yet decided. Joan wanted to let Killeen for the winter and the spring, but it was difficult to find a tenant who wanted that. It was possible to let in the spring, and easy to let for the spring, summer and autumn. They left the matter in their factor's hands with instructions to keep them informed of any offers. Countess San Felice and the Cantillons came to stay with them while they were in Scotland, and they saw a great many people. Joan saw nothing of Alexander, but she was told by her aunt that he was doing very well in the House of Commons, and when she asked whether he was married, her aunt said that he was much smitten by a beautiful and attractive American lady, the wife of one of the American diplomats.

When they got back to Malta at the beginning of November they found there was a new Lieutenant-Governor. His name was Wilfrid Childs. He had been a distinguished traveller and was a Fellow of All Souls. He was a Persian and Arabic scholar. He was a large man, rather bald, with Roman features, grey hair and a silvery voice and a courtly manner; and he had lived so long in the East that he had acquired some of the celestial serenity of the oriental. His wife was the daughter of Keely, the celebrated portrait painter. She herself greatly resembled a picture, but her beauty belonged less to the Victorian epoch than to that of Sir Thomas Lawrence: Lawrence and Greuze were the two painters she called to mind, and she would have been labelled British School rather than French.

She had brown hair, blue eyes and a transparent complexion. She was much younger than her husband, and there were no children. She made friends with the Keiths at once. She had a sunny nature, a crystal laugh and, at times, flashes of a rather malicious wit.

Her mother had been noted for her sudden paroxysms of nerve storms, her soft eyes, her languishing airs and graces and her sharp sayings. She had not been a month in Malta before Robert Keith was her devoted slave. But Beryl Childs was careful to rope Joan into her friendship with Robert. She saw Joan constantly: took her out driving, consulted her about her parties, her house and her garden; lent her books; went out sketching with her. But in spite of this, Joan, although she said she liked Mrs Childs, did not accord her a particle of real intimacy. She was delighted that Robert should have a friend, and slightly irritated at the almost religious awe with which he regarded Beryl.

It was the general opinion that Mrs Childs was not only a charming but a good woman; some people went so far as to say a *saint:* so considerate, so unselfish, and so untiring in good works. She fulfilled her official duties admirably, and she was greatly liked by the various societies of the island. Joan thought there was a great deal to admire in Beryl Childs; but as for saying she was a saint, she knew from having known her sister-in-law what saints, real saints, were like, and that to call Beryl Childs one was ridiculous.

Gradually Joan became aware that Beryl was exercising a subtle, an almost invisible but paramount influence over Robert. Just before Christmas Joan received a letter from the factor saying that someone had made an offer to take Killeen for two years.

Joan discussed the matter with Robert.

'We needn't accept it,' she said; 'you would like to go to England in the summer.'

'It wouldn't prevent us from going to England,' said Robert. 'Let's think it over for a day.'

It happened to be a Saturday afternoon, and they went to the races. The Childs' were there and Beryl talked for some time to Robert. Joan had asked one or two midshipmen to tea, and when these had left, Robert said to Joan:

'I think we had better accept that offer. I shan't go back to England this summer. Of course you can always go if you want to.'

'If we can afford it,' said Joan, 'I should like to have Killeen to go to in the summer.'

'Oh, we can afford it perfectly,' said Robert. 'We have been very good, you know.'

The next day, in the course of a casual conversation, Beryl Childs told Joan that she and her husband were not going to England in the summer but were going to stay in the island. That evening, when Joan and Robert were in their sitting-room, just before dinner – they were dining out and it was almost dressing-time – Joan said to Robert:

'I am going to write to Macfarlane and tell him to refuse that offer.'

'You want to go to Scotland in the summer?'

'Yes,' said Joan, 'and I want to take the children, but you could stay here.'

'Yes,' said Robert, 'I could stay here.'

And Joan thought at first that he was pleased with the idea, though he said nothing. That night they dined at the Governor's, and Robert sat next to Beryl Childs, and, although Joan was on the other side of the table and some distance off, she was acutely conscious that he was telling Beryl the news.

'There is no doubt about it,' she thought to herself. 'He loves her, and she loves him even more than he loves her.'

Joan was sitting next to Wilfrid Childs, and he was explaining to her that when the Persians used the word 'wine' they often meant the Spirit of God.

But when the spring came and Joan discussed her summer plans with Robert, and said she wanted to go to England, Robert said:

'Are you really going to leave me all alone, without the children even?'

'Why don't you come with me?' said Joan.

It was a brilliant morning in April. They were sitting out of doors in the little square full of plants which was in front of their house. The children were playing. And the baby was sleeping in the perambulator.

'I don't want to come to England,' he said; 'I feel so out of it there now, and I think the summer here is so jolly, and I thought we would have such fun here this year – all of us together. The Childs' are going to be here all the summer. She was saying only the other day that it would spoil everything if you were not here. Do stay.'

Joan understood what was the truth, that he did want her to stay. He liked them all to be together: herself, Robert and the Childs'.

'I'm not sure he is in love with her,' she thought, 'but she is in love with him.'

It was finally settled that she would not go to Scotland that year, and she wrote to the factor and told him to try and let Killeen for the summer or autumn, or both. Joan resigned herself to the prospect of seeing the Childs' every day of her life.

It was towards the end of May that Joan fell ill. It was Malta fever, and she was ill for two months. When she got well the doctor said positively she must get away out of the island, so Robert took her to England at the end of July, and they went to Killeen, which was not let. The Childs came to England too, for a short time, and Robert said that of course they must be asked to Killeen, Wilfrid Childs was so fond of shooting. They were invited, and arrived at the end of August. The Cantillons and Countess San Felice were there already.

Mrs Childs sat next to Horace Cantillon at dinner the night they arrived. The Baillies were there and some other neighbours. It was quite a dinner-party. Joan was at the other end of the table, well out of hearing, so Mrs Childs began to pour into Horace Cantillon's ear a long and subtle eulogy of Joan.

'I don't know what we should do without her at Malta,' she said, 'she simply transforms the place for us, I think. She makes everyone else there seem dead. And she is good to everyone. She remembers to ask everyone, even the most tiresome people. I wish I could be like that. Wilfrid often tells me that if only I were like Joan his career would be made.'

'I'm afraid the climate of Malta doesn't suit her,' said Horace Cantillon. 'It's a pity, as it suits Robert down to the ground.'

'I think,' said Beryl, 'that it's only in summer that it disagrees with her. She is quite well in the winter. The ideal thing would be for her to spend the summers in England.'

'Well, I think that's what will happen. I was anxious when she was ill this year,' he went on; 'one never knows what sort of doctor one will get hold of in those outlandish places.'

'Well, Joan had the great good fortune to discover an excellent doctor, a Maltese called Valea. He was entirely her discovery. He really did wonders for her. I believe he is a most charming man, at least so everyone says. I hardly know him; I have only just met him. Wilfrid is so insular and insists on being looked after by the English doctor, but I must say that Dr Valea appreciates Joan. He understood at once what a wonderful person she is. As you must know better than anyone, Joan never puts herself forward. She always deliberately keeps in the background, so that unless people make an effort they would

178

never guess what a remarkable person she is. Wilfrid guessed at once; so did I. We said to each other the day we met her, the first time we set eyes on her, "That is really someone, something rare." Of course the average inhabitant of Malta has no idea what she is like really. If one talks about her they say, "Mrs Keith? Oh yes, she's so nice, rather *foreign* and rather shy."'

Horace Cantillon loved hearing all that, and he said to his wife, when the Childs', the Keiths and the others had gone, some upstairs and some to smoke:

'That Mrs Childs is a charming woman; and how good-looking!'

'Her mother was affected,' said Mrs Cantillon.

'She reminds one of an Italian picture – a Raphael or a Correggio,' said Horace.

'Yes, she means to remind you of a Madonna,' said Countess San Felice, 'but she is a minx all the same. And she is the kind of woman men swallow whole.'

'Well, she appreciates Joan, that's one thing, and it must be everything,' said Horace, 'for Joan and Robert to have someone like that at Malta.'

'Oh, everything,' said the Countess, looking meaningly at Mrs Cantillon.

'Let us go to bed, Amy dear,' and as they went upstairs she whispered to her:

'*Que les hommes sont bêtes.*'

'Yes, indeed!' said Mrs Cantillon. 'Poor Joan!'

Countess San Felice went up to Joan's bedroom. She found Mrs Childs there, who, after a little while, tactfully said she must go to bed.

'Your uncle is quite in love with her,' said Countess San Felice.

'And so is Robert,' said Joan.

'She could never take Robert away from you,' said Countess San Felice. 'It is she that loves him, not he that loves her.'

'Yes, but he finds her a comfort. She is a great comfort to us all.'

'Who is that doctor she says you have discovered and like so much?'

Joan laughed.

'She told you that, did she? It's Dr Valea, a Maltese. He's very clever and he cured me. But you needn't be alarmed. He's nearly seventy, a widower, with children.'

CHAPTER 14

The Childs' stayed at Killeen ten days. They went back to Malta at the end of September. Joan and Robert followed a little later.

Dr Valea came to see Joan the day she arrived, to inquire after her health. He was a short man, and had been dark, but his hair was now white; he had soft, penetrating, kind eyes, and a charming voice. He had studied in Italy and Germany, taken many degrees, and written books and pamphlets that were famous in Europe on malarial and other diseases. He was interested in Joan, but it was her mental state rather than the state of her physical health that interested him. She was giving him tea in the little room.

He had got to know her well during her illness, both as a patient and as a human being, and he was beginning to know her still better when he had insisted on her going to England. But now, after this break of a few weeks only, they both felt, when they met again, that they were on a new and different footing of intimacy; it was as if their friendship had matured and ripened during their separation. Joan felt there was nothing she would mind saying to Dr Valea now.

'And how is Colonel Keith?' he asked.

'He is very well. He has gone out riding, and he said he would not be back till after tea.'

Joan had said she would be not at home to any visitors except the doctor. She wanted to speak to him. She had carried on so many imaginary conversations with him during his absence.

'And was your stay in England successful and agreeable?'

'I was glad to be there. I love Scotland, but Robert doesn't really like it. He was happy this year,' she said pensively, 'at least for a part of the time.'

'There was the sport.'

'Robert doesn't like fishing and doesn't much care for shooting; at least not that kind of shooting. And then it's too cold for him. He's always cold in Scotland. He likes to spend the summer in a place where it's not necessary to have a fire in the evening.'

'Like Malta.'

'Yes, like Malta I oughtn't to have let him come to England. I shan't let him come next year. I have arranged to let my house for three years. I did it once before. I am sometimes a little anxious about him even here.'

'But it is good for *you* to be in England every now and then.'

'It doesn't matter, Dr Valea, in the least where I am.'

'Why do you say that?'

'Because it's true. I matter a little to the children, not so much as their nanny, but I matter to no one else.'

'I think your husband is completely lost without you.'

'I used to think so too, but I'm not sure. I'm not sure I ought to have married him. Not because I haven't loved him. I have. I did and I do love him, and he did love me and he does still, in a sort of way. But underneath all that the differences are too great.'

'Aren't they always?'

'I don't think so. In the first place, you see, Robert is a practising Catholic and I am a worse than bad Catholic, a Catholic only in name.'

'Yes, I see Colonel Keith at Mass.'

'You go to Mass?'

'Every day, if possible.'

'In spite of all your science?'

'Science only teaches one how little one knows: that one knows nothing; and whatever one learns, one learns, too, that there is a margin for the unknown; the unknowable; the Divine.'

'I wish I could feel like that, but I can't. I am like the bad soil on which the grain fell; there is not even the excuse of thorns – just nothing; no soil.'

'I believe you expect too much of belief, you want to think things *probable*.'

'I can't be like the man – one of the Fathers – who said he believed because it was impossible.'

'That was only said as a telling exaggeration.'

'Oh, I understand *that*. You needn't explain. It's just what I should have liked to have said myself. But how can one know? How can anyone know? I can't help thinking that people believe what they want to believe. Catholics believe in their faith and are ready to die for it, but so do Buddhists and Mohammedans, and so do all kinds of Calvinists.'

'But apart from dying for them, would you find those creeds you have mentioned worth living for and with? Does Mohammedan morality satisfy you? Do you find the Buddhist hope of being one day absorbed and merged into the nothingness inspires you? Does the cat-and-mouse pouncing God of Calvinism attract and command your belief?'

'No, they don't, but I can't help thinking that the Buddhist creed is the reflection of what people who are Buddhists want, just as the Mohammedan Paradise of Houris is the reflection of what the Arabs think ideal, and the Calvinist doctrine the reflection of that

184

terrible dour Genevan temperament.'

'Yes, but what is the Catholic Church the reflection of? I believe there is only one answer: the universal and the Divine. You see it is so big and so all-embracing that no one can even *say* it is the reflection of this or that temperament, or this or that continent, race or country. It embraces them all; all other creeds are either what Newman calls 'Seeds of Truth', hints and prophecies of its truth, or distortions of its truth, or warped and lopped branches. And if human life is divine in its origin, and not an accident, and it must be one or the other, and if this Divinity has been attested by Divine Revelation, there can only be One Truth and One Authority on earth to represent it and interpret it.'

'Yes; but what about people like my father who disbelieved in Revelation altogether?'

'Renan, when he tells us about the laceration leaving the Church cost him, says that in reality very few people have the right to disbelieve in Christianity. They don't know how strong and solid the arguments for it are. But of course if you do admit Revelation other things follow of necessity: everything down to Holy Water and Scapulars, as St Teresa, I think, said, and Renan saw so clearly; and if you don't accept Revelation, and if you at the same time don't believe life is an accident, if you believe in a God, as I assume you do, you are forced to construct

185

some third philosophy based on natural religion. Personally I am unable to do that. Such philosophies don't satisfy me.'

'In England I have so often heard people say that it doesn't in the least matter what Church one goes to, or whether one worships in a church or in a field, so long as one worships in spirit and in truth.'

'That *is* what is called natural religion, and it is all right as far as it goes; but if you believe in *Revelation*, as Catholics do, you then believe in supernatural religion, and that leads you willy-nilly to certain other conclusions, such as the Church, infallible authority, etc.'

'Yes, that is just what my father used to say. You see, he pointed out to me the errors of all the heresies and the weak points of all the philosophies; but he gave me nothing instead, nothing to put in their place, except an interest in the Catholic Church, which he looked upon with a kind of respectful scepticism. I know what the Catholic Church teaches is, so far as I know it, *different* and reasonable, and it always seems to me that if you go inside a Catholic Church it is unlike any other building, and especially any other church, or mosque, or temple. Perhaps the truth is I am too ignorant. I went to a priest once, and all he told me was to pray. That's just what I can't do.'

'It's a gift, but one never knows when it

may come. When I was a young man I discarded all religious belief for about five years, till my eldest son was born and died. It was his death, not his birth, that brought me back. Sorrow built a bridge for me into the infinite. It often does. You, perhaps, have never experienced sorrow?'

'I thought I did when my father died. But it brought me nothing but a sense of desolation. I felt as if everything in the world had been swept and blasted by a dry whirl-wind, and I had been left alone in a barren place.'

'One has to *accept* sorrow for it to be of any healing power, and that is the most difficult thing in the world.'

'I didn't think about it in that way. I don't think I rebelled against it, because I thought my father was happier dead and at peace, than alive and in pain; but I was just stunned. Apart from that, I have not experienced real sorrow; only disappointment and disillusion.'

'A priest once said to me, "When you understand what *accepted* sorrow means, you will understand everything. It is the secret of life." It is true. Dante knew that and expressed it in one line. The same priest said, "Wisdom is everywhere all round us, but hidden." We must look for it. But we are afraid of looking and asking.'

'That is why I am asking you. I want to be taught.'

'I am the wrong person to ask.'

'It's no good my going to the professionals. They do not understand where I am, nor what I mean. They think I am bothered with points that I have never given a thought to; that I boggle at this or that dogma, or at this or that custom or rite. They don't see that if I believed with my *heart* in the first sentences of the Creed I would accept all the rest, down to the Scapulars and Holy Water – as you said – without questioning. I read, I think, in Newman's *Apologia* that a thousand difficulties don't make a doubt. I have got no difficulties, but huge doubts. Or else they think that I believe in the agnostics, philosophers and materialists, in George Eliot and Renan. I don't. My father taught me not to. Or that I am an Oriental pessimist. I'm quite ready not to be. I have found no one who can help, but books do help. I like reading about these things. But I am so ignorant. I have never been taught anything. That's what makes it so difficult. They all take it for granted – Robert included – that I have been taught everything, and I know nothing; I have been taught nothing. I want to be taught. Can't you teach me?'

'How can I teach you? I think it is a mistake to go to laymen to be taught in these matters, just as it is a mistake to consult laymen on matters of medicine. It is perhaps a mistake to discuss this matter at all. I have always found that it is impossible to discuss the Catholic Church with anyone except Catholics. It only leads to misunderstanding and quarrel, and among English people if you do it you are suspected of 'propaganda'. It is a subject that eliminates impartiality. But I am sure of one thing. I can teach you nothing. Whatever one knows and learns, whatever and however sincerely one believes, the mysteries remain mysteries, and I cannot get beyond saying, "Lord, I believe, help Thou my unbelief."'

'I wish I could get as far as saying that. That is all I want and all I ask.'

'The only people who can teach one are not the clever people but the good. Not the so-called "good", but the really good – the saints.'

'I am sure you are right: but where are they?'

'They are everywhere. One comes across them by accident.'

'I sometimes think,' said Joan, 'that people who I think are saints wear strange masks, and that at the last day we shall have some great surprises, and see many so-called goats numbered with the sheep.'

'Yes – indeed.'

'But then such people often have no religious belief: nothing definite, that is to say.'

'They often have been taught nothing. Religious teaching hasn't come their way.

189

It's not their fault. It's the fault of the way of the world.'

'Yes, but it's no good my going to such people to be taught religion. I can profit by their example; but as for the theory, they have none to teach.'

'Some people have both. Hundreds of *curés* and not very literate parish priests behave like saints and reason like angels.'

'Oh, they reason too well! What can all the reason in the world do, if one doesn't believe? I don't want reason. I have been fed on reason all my life. My father was reasonable, and he taught me all that reason has to say; but at the same time he was careful to tell me that I must never trust reason; never think it infallible. My first husband was clever, and he was profoundly sceptical and didn't believe in anything; he was good at heart, but his whole life was ruined, and partly by me; first, by a fatal passion for a woman of genius who didn't love him, who loved someone else; and then, when he married me, I ought to have made things right. I ought to have filled his life; but I didn't; I was too proud at first. I couldn't forgive him for loving the other woman. But later I did, only it was too late. Instead of being useful I was useless – and then he died. And then I married Robert; and Robert is a saint in many ways. He has never thought of not believing. He imbibed faith as a child, and it has never left him. He has never questioned it for a moment. He takes it for granted that nobody who has been born and baptized a Catholic could ever question it. That is why I am such a puzzle to him – worse than a puzzle – a disappointment; and that is why I am terribly afraid my second marriage may turn out to be just as great a failure as my first; because underneath all Robert's love for me and all his affection there is a bar and a difference, and I think he feels that I am wanting; and I *am* wanting, and I can't help it; and he feels, I am sure, that I shall not be capable of bringing up the children right.'

'I think you are bringing up your children admirably.'

'Andrew is going to be like his father, and Antony, as far as one can tell – he's only four – will be like me, and Kathleen – I don't know – I only know she is a naughty baby. I have taught them what my nurse taught me. They are too small to ask the difficult questions; but when they do I don't know what I shall answer. My father couldn't answer the questions I used to ask him.'

'The best answers to the riddle of life are in the Penny Catechism, and that is a fact that struck the most sceptical philosophers; they admit that the explanation of the universe given by the Catechism is more satisfactory than anything devised by Plato, Aristotle, Spinoza or Kant.'

'I don't feel capable of teaching what I know so little myself.'

'The boys will go to school, I suppose?'

'Oh yes, Robert is sending them to the Oratory, where he was at school, and I must find a governess for Andrew this winter. He's six years old. In three years' time he will be going to school, and I'm not capable of teaching him enough to be ready for that. He knows how to read already: he won't be clever, but he will be painstaking.'

'You will be able to find a good governess here, and I don't think it much matters what boys are taught in the way of book-learning till they get to school; they will be well taught at the Oratory. As for Kathleen, you will find that daughters teach themselves.'

'Yes, but what I am afraid of is that I may be a hindrance instead of a help, as I was to my first husband.'

'How do you know you were?'

'I did nothing to help him. He was terribly in need of help. His life was empty. I might have filled it, but I didn't. I remained obstinately aloof from him – as I told you – until it was too late.'

'And the other woman?'

'She went into a convent and died soon after. She was Dorzan, the actress.'

'Oh! Dorzan!'

'You knew her?'

'I saw her act often in Italy and in Paris, and I knew a lot about her. She was a great genius. I understand. I had, of course, no idea of what you have just told me.'

There was a pause.

'You know,' Joan said, after a while, 'she married?'

'Yes.'

'But what you perhaps didn't know is that my husband, Glencairn, was wildly in love with her and had always wanted to marry her, and she had sworn to him that she loved no one and was leaving the stage to take the veil.'

'She probably meant to at the time.'

'She may have meant to; but she married an Italian, Alfredo Chiaromonte.'

'I know; but all the same I don't believe Dorzan loved any man; although men loved her desperately; she perhaps loved her art – unconsciously; it possessed her like a fever and it killed her. That is why, when she said she wanted to be a nun, it was probably true.'

'You know the rest of the story?'

'Her husband was shot by accident.'

'Yes, by my husband.'

There was another long pause, and Joan looked at Valea. Then she knew at once that he knew what had happened: the whole truth; and that they were for ever bound and linked together by the bond of an immense silent confidence that would never need expression or explanation. And at that moment Robert Keith came into the room.

CHAPTER 15

After the conversation described in the last chapter, the intimacy between Joan and Valea had reached a new and indeed a final stage. That is to say, it never increased after that because it had already gone as far as it could go. Joan felt that Valea knew and understood exactly what her life had been; that he knew all that mattered; that what he did not know were only details that might or might not be filled in, but which had no great significance.

Just after Christmas they were thrown together by Robert's falling ill with pneumonia. Valea looked after him and Joan nursed him. He was seriously ill until the end of January, and then was a long time convalescing. At one moment they feared for his life, and Joan sat up nursing him day and night. He received the last sacraments. He was conscious, and did not seem to be in the least afraid of death or reluctant to leave the world. He seemed content, serene and a little dazed, and to be meeting death with the faith of a child. Joan had never felt fonder of him and never less capable of sharing his faith. He, Valea, and the priest who was with him, moved in what for her was an alien and a forbidden world. She longed to be in it with them. She knew it was impossible. She had tried. Under Valea's guidance she had read a great deal of theology. She had discussed religious topics with Robert's priest, a learned French Jesuit, to whom she explained that if she was to have a good influence on her children she must have a groundwork of knowledge. She studied Church history. She read Renan, Newman and Dante. It all interested her greatly, but it brought her no nearer the possibility of opening the gate and walking in. The grain of faith no greater than a mustard seed eluded her; but she still hoped that some day it might, by some unforeseen accident, or rather some providential design, fall into her heart. She knew that at present it would not. She no longer discussed her doubts with Valea, but she often talked to him about the history of the Church and discussed points of moral theology and dogma; but they always ended by his referring her to a priest and pleading ignorance, in spite of what seemed to be his immense store of knowledge. She felt that he could understand her better than any priest could. Joan had been brought nearer to Robert by his illness than she had ever been before; and she thought to herself that when he was well again their married life would take on a new lease, and that they would be happier together and understand each other better than ever before. But directly Robert was well again, which was in the spring, he seemed to see more of the Childs', and less of Joan than ever.

Beryl Childs, during his illness, had behaved with tact and discretion. She had called to inquire every day; had sent flowers when he was better; but she had not pestered Joan nor put herself too much forward.

Then came the summer, and the old question of how and where they were to spend it. Joan had always wanted to go to Scotland before, but this year she would have gladly stayed at Malta. Killeen was not let, but Joan had taken it for granted they would let it for the summer if they got an offer, as Robert, she thought, would certainly not want to go there.

The matter was brought to a head one morning by a letter coming from the factor telling Joan of an offer that had been made by some foreigners to take Killeen for August and September: the factor asked Joan to cable the answer. Joan showed the letter to Robert and said:

'We had better accept the offer, hadn't we?'

'Oh, do you think so?' said Robert. 'I thought it would do us both good to go to Scotland this year.'

'You don't want to stay here?' said Joan.

'Not the whole summer.'

'Very well, I will cable and tell Macfarlane we won't let.'

'Yes,' said Robert, 'that leaves us free. We needn't go if we don't want to; but if we do, Killeen will be there ready for us. It will do the children good to get some fresh air.'

Joan sent off a cable, but she said in it, 'Sending answer tomorrow', as before deciding not to let Killeen she wanted the doctor's opinion as to where Robert should spend the summer. As she was walking from the office of the Eastern Telegraph she met Beryl Childs.

'You are just the person I wanted to see,' said Beryl. 'I have got a piece of news for you. Wilfrid's uncle has lent him his house in Scotland for August and September; it's called "Laracor", and I believe it's not far from you.'

'Only ten miles,' said Joan.

'Well, that will be delightful. You and Robert must come and stay with us: that is to say, if you are going to Scotland.'

'We are probably going,' said Joan. 'I have just sent a cable about it.'

'I'm so glad. I thought you might have been staying here this summer. I thought Dr Valea might have recommended it to Robert.'

'I don't know what Dr Valea thinks yet,'

said Joan. 'I haven't asked him, but I expect he will think it good for Robert to have a change.'

'Well, I hope he does. What fun it will be! I attribute it entirely to dear St Anthony. I was longing to go to Scotland this year, but I didn't see how we could manage it, so I thought I would put up a candle in the church round the corner – it's his church, you know – and ask St Anthony to arrange it for me. I didn't quite know how to do it, so I got that nice Father Hallaway to do it for me, and they put up a huge candle near the altar; and a week after Wilfrid got his uncle's letter. I didn't tell Wilfrid about the candle because he has no patience with my little superstitions, but I know *you* understand, Joan darling, and I always say that although you were brought up as a Roman you make me feel how little difference there is between us all and how we all believe the same thing *really;* anyhow I am sure St Anthony doesn't mind my little offerings as he *always* finds the things I lose when I ask him; but this is the very best thing he has *ever* done for me; I am longing for Robert to know.'

Joan was convinced that Robert knew already, which was indeed the truth: at least Beryl had told him some days before that they hoped to spend their leave in England. Nothing irritated Joan more than Beryl's sentimental patronage of the Catholic saints and Catholic custom, practice and ritual; but all she said was:

'We so want you and Wilfrid to come to dinner on Sunday night.'

Beryl said they would be delighted, and then she left Joan. She was going to Admiralty House.

For a moment Joan almost made up her mind that nothing would induce her to go to England this summer. Robert could go by himself, and she would stay in Malta. But after a moment she said to herself:

'God give me sense.'

She went home and wrote a note to Dr Valea, telling him she was anxious to see him as soon as possible and alone, as she wanted to discuss Robert's health. Dr Valea sent her an answer saying he would be in his house at half past five, but had to go to the hospital later. Joan arrived and he gave her tea in his funny little formal drawing-room, which was furnished with red silk chairs and full of oil-paintings in large gilt frames, and some bookshelves filled with unbound medical books and pamphlets in many languages. Joan attacked the subject immediately.

'Ought Robert to spend the summer here or in England?'

'It doesn't matter,' the doctor said; 'whichever he fancies, but he ought to be back here in October. He must by no means spend the winter in England. I'm not sure that even

Malta is not too cold for him.'

'He wants to go to England,' said Joan.

'And you will go too?'

'I suppose so.'

'You must – it will do you good. It is bad for you to spend the summer here.'

'Life is so puzzling,' said Joan. 'When I wanted to be in England in summer Robert didn't, and now, when I don't want to go, he does.'

'Don't you want to go?'

'Not this year. Robert doesn't want me.'

'Are you sure?'

'Quite sure.'

'You must go all the same. He wants looking after.'

'You're not anxious about him?'

'He's perfectly well at present, but he's always liable to get something in that lung – on the whole I think it will do him good to go.'

'He would go, whatever you said. It is the first time he has ever really *wanted* to go.'

'I am going away too, this summer,' said Valea.

'To England?'

'No, to Italy, to Sorrento.'

'For the summer?'

'No – for good.'

'Oh!' said Joan, and she felt suddenly as if the world had gone dark and chill. '*Not for good?*' she repeated.

'It's like this,' he said, 'one of my daughters married an Italian, a lawyer, who was very well-known, called Alessandri. They have got four children. I had a cable last week from her saying that her husband was dead, and today I got a letter begging me to come out and live with her; she cannot face life by herself; and it's true. He did everything for her.'

'But after a time, when she has got over the first sharpness of her sorrow – and one does get over it – when she has settled down with the rest of life again – and one does settle down – won't you come back?'

'No. I don't think I shall ever come back. My daughter is too old to begin life over again, and I haven't much more time to live. I shan't have time to come back.'

'You know what this means to me.'

'It means a great deal to me as well. It is life.'

'Yes, it is life. I have made few friends in my life; hardly any; but directly I have made one something has always happened to put an end to the friendships. When are you going?'

'At once.'

Joan said nothing.

'We will write to each other. Letters are not the best thing, but they are the second best.'

'And who knows? we may meet again in

Italy. Unfortunately Robert doesn't like Italy. He will miss you too; there will be nobody here to look after him.'

'Smythson, my pupil, is clever: but it is you who will look after your husband better than anyone else.'

'It is a curious thing,' said Joan, 'that one should be most severely punished when one has done what one thinks right. When I was a girl I was in love with a man called Alexander Luttrell and he loved me. Then there was a misunderstanding and a series of mistakes; and he became engaged to my cousin, Agatha Cantillon, whom I was very fond of. Then Lord Glencairn proposed to me and I accepted him; immediately after that, the misunderstanding between me and Alexander, which had brought about all the trouble, was cleared up by accident. It would not have been too late for both of us to have broken off our engagements, and we could have married. Alexander would have been ready to do it. I positively refused. I thought it would break Agatha's heart, which it would have done. But looking back on it now, were we right? I'm not sure. You see, they married, went to India, and she died after a miscarriage. He is in politics; he has not married again; he's no children, and I'm told he's more or less the *cavaliere servente* of an American lady – a lonely, dull existence. What did I achieve by doing what

I thought was right and my duty? I ruined Glencairn's life and Dorzan's, because if I hadn't married Glencairn it is possible she wouldn't have married Chiaromonte.'

'Put that out of your head. She knew nothing about your marriage when she married Chiaromonte. He is the only man she would ever have married.'

'How do you know that?'

'Because, although I believe she loved no one, he was her lover. She owed him everything; she was obliged to marry him.'

'All the same it made it worse for Glencairn being married to me – and our marriage wasn't a marriage – so what was the use?'

'Any man who loved Dorzan must have been like a patient afflicted with a terrible incurable fever and needing the tenderest and most intelligent and subtle medical care. I expect you supplied that.'

'I didn't until it was too late. I did my best – at the end – when he was ill – about to die, although we didn't know it. He died from a fall – walking in his sleep. We understood each other. I think I was, in those few days between the accident and his own death, of some help and comfort to him.'

'That is exactly what I meant and what I supposed, and that is the kind of thing one is sent into life to do. I am an old man, my life is nearly over, but it is not quite over yet. And now, at the eleventh hour, I am given a new task. I have to begin all over again: to go to a new country and to look after my daughter and her children. But you are young.'

'I am thirty-one,' interrupted Joan.

'That is very young. I am more than twice your age. You have had much to do already, but you will have a great deal more. Besides, your husband and your children–'

'Don't,' said Joan. 'My life has been and always will be entirely negative. I have no faith in anything.'

'It may seem negative to you, but it may be positive for other people – like a picture that to one eye only seems a blur of smudges but to another is an ordered pattern of symmetrical colour. Or like a stained-glass window, which to you on the wrong side of it is dark and meaningless, but to me on the right side of it is a glory of design and colour. Your life has made a positive note in mine, and it may be positive to many others.' The doctor looked at his watch. 'It is late,' he said. 'I shall have to be going. I've got to see someone at Bighi.'

'I can drive you there,' said Joan.

'Drive me to the Customs House steps,' he said, 'and I'll take a dghaisa. I shan't have time to drive round.'

Joan took the doctor in her victoria. They drove down to the Customs House in silence most of the way. They got to the waterfront

205

and walked along the road to get a dghaisa. Joan, as she looked round her, said:

'It will all be different. You must write to me often; I shall have no one to talk to.'

'The life sentence,' he said, 'of every mortal soul is solitary confinement.'

'Yes; but you have your faith like sunshine beyond the bars.'

'The sunshine is there. Even if you don't feel it. You must try and take that on trust from others. Do you really want more evidence than that? Look,' and he pointed to the setting sun.

'I do take it on trust, but I long to feel it myself. I am so cold – so very cold – in spite of all that.'

She too pointed to the west. The sun was setting in glory in an azure sky, in which there were a few sulphurous and soft-purple clouds fringed with fire. The blue water was flecked with a thousand reflections from the orange sun-baked houses and the green shutters, and here and there the coloured sails and green hulls of the Gozo boats; dghaisas were skimming like coloured toy gondolas across the water; the boatmen shouting at each other with guttural, shrill objurgations. One or two picket-boats steamed by, making a wash. The bells were ringing from the church towers. The bugles on board all the men-of-war sounded sunset; and the whole world seemed to stand to attention with the sailors. The ships supplied a note of stern reality; and with their noble lines, their light grey paint, their dark shadows, their formidable guns, and all their serene evidence of silent power, they blent magnificently and, as it were, inevitably with the fantastic and glowing background, the sun-gilded masonry, the tawny walls, the russet sails, the rainbow-coloured waters; a background and a scene which might have been chosen by the fancy of Shakespeare in which to set another comedy as full of sunshine as *Twelfth Night*, or another tragedy as sombre as *Othello;* a background which he dreamt of, possibly, but which remained among unsorted and rejected heaps of 'unvalued stones' in the infinite treasury of his mind.

When the ceremony of sunset was over on board the ships and the flags were all hauled down, Valea said to Joan:

'It's a beautiful world, isn't it?'

'Yes,' said Joan, 'a beautiful world, but a very sad one. Goodbye.'

'Good night,' said the doctor as he got into his dghaisa.

Joan stood watching the little boat speed quickly over the many-coloured water, until it was hidden by a big ship.

She never saw him again.

CHAPTER 16

It was settled the next day that Joan and Robert should go to Scotland for the summer, and Joan's factor was instructed to refuse the let of Killeen. Dr Valea left two days after the meeting with Joan described in the last chapter. He called on Joan and Robert when they were out and left two cards with 'PPC' on them.

Joan and Robert and the children and Signorina Carpi left for England at the end of June, and after a week in London went straight to Scotland. The Childs' did not come to Scotland until the 12th of August. Robert went to shoot with them, but Joan stayed at Killeen with the children. Andrew was growing up like his father; Antony like his mother; and Kathleen, who was now three years old, seemed to Joan to be a changeling. Signorina Carpi, the governess, had been with them a year. She had been found for Joan by her aunt, Countess San Felice. She was a Florentine, and an enthusiastic lover of all branches of art; she and a sister had been left destitute by their father, an artist who had been a great friend of the Countess. She had taken the elder sister into her house and arranged for the second, Maria, to be governess to Joan's children. She was about thirty: simple, cultivated and enthusiastic; a pious Catholic, and she taught the children Italian and French, which she knew well. Joan was delighted with her, and especially pleased that she was capable of undertaking the religious instruction of the children, which she felt incapable of doing. She did not go into the question of her own beliefs and disbeliefs with the Signorina, but she made it clear she wished them taught what Catholics should believe; she confined herself to hearing them say their prayers. Later on at school the boys would receive religious instruction in plenty.

They hadn't been long in Scotland before Joan got news from her Aunt Amy that Horace Cantillon was seriously ill. She went south at once, leaving the children with the Signorina. Robert was at Laracor, where he stayed during all Joan's absence. Horace Cantillon died a few days after her arrival, and Joan stayed on with her aunt till the end of August, and then took her back with her to Scotland. She made this an excuse for neither asking the Childs' to stay at Killeen nor going to Laracor herself.

At the end of September the Childs' were due back at Malta. Robert stayed with them once more before they left. Then in October Joan and Robert, the children and the Sig-

210

norina, all went south and sailed for Malta.

When Joan got back to Malta she found she missed Dr Valea immensely. He wrote to her regularly and she wrote to him, but Malta without him seemed a different place.

She persuaded Countess San Felice to come out in the winter, and she stayed with them for Christmas and the month of January.

Life settled down for Joan into a mechanical routine. She asked the same people to luncheon and dinner; sailors and soldiers came to tea; they went to watch the polo; they went to the races on Saturday; there were parties and sometimes dances on board the ships; dinners and luncheons at the Governor's, who sometimes had distinguished guests staying with him, or at other times invited distinguished travellers who were passing through. The Childs' they saw nearly every day. Joan went through the whole of the social round quite automatically. She felt she had never done anything else. She was liked by the English people, but not understood. 'Of course,' people would say, 'she's half foreign, and that accounts for it.' By 'it' they meant probably a profound fundamental indifference to the doings and opinions of other people, a reserved manner, mixed with moments and outbursts of frankness and directness of speech to which they were not used and which the English ladies excused as being 'so Italian'. The Maltese society found Joan entirely delightful, and had no difficulty in understanding her; nor had the midshipmen who came to tea with her. They got on with her and found her great fun. It was the senior officers' wives who were some of them critical and said they pitied poor Colonel Keith because Mrs Keith was so unsociable and did so little, whereas he would be so sociable and would enjoy seeing people, if she would let him. No wonder he went so much to the Childs'. Mrs Childs was a woman who understood what life in a place like Malta should be.

But Joan was indifferent to what the people around her thought or said. She felt she had already been two people in her life, and that now she was a third. She saw no relation between herself and the callow girl-companion of her elderly and clever father or the wife of Glencairn, or even between what she was now and what she had been during the first years of her marriage to Robert. Her intimacy with Dr Valea had been for her like the brilliant stripe in a spectrum, and she thought this was an element which was going to make a permanent difference in her life. It did, but not in the way she had expected. His sudden and final departure put an end to the companionship she had hoped for, and which she had indeed begun to taste; but the friendship, although it lasted in actual companionship such a short time, had a durable and permanent effect upon Joan. It had opened doors for her and changed her outlook, and the letters which passed between them maintained for her a private life, a series of adventures in which the soul took part and which were separate from her daily life and unsuspected by anyone. She knew she would never see Dr Valea again, but she was not sure it was not better so. He was almost more living to her in the letters which she received from him, for their correspondence went on like an unending chain; when he wrote to her she wrote back to him. Joan had entirely ceased to be jealous of Beryl Childs; and she noticed with some amusement that Beryl's husband, Wilfrid, who at one moment had shown signs of jealousy, had ceased to be jealous too. She remained on perfectly good terms with Beryl: the most she felt against her was a slight irritation, which she suppressed. It could not but be a little provoking to know that Beryl was five years younger than she was and that Robert believed every word she said. Then she had the children. They played a new and all-important part in her life. By the time Andrew, the eldest, was seven years old, Joan saw that he was going to take strongly after his father. He was a serious, thoughtful little boy and, contrary to Joan's expectations, he asked her no puzzling theological questions. He seemed to accept what he was taught without difficulty. Antony was a little imp, full of mischief and fun. He was fair and had blue eyes, taking after Joan's father. He was for ever getting into mischief, and as soon as he could manifest anything he gave expression to a passion for ships and the sea, and boats of every description. Kathleen showed evidence when she was still a baby of Joan's Italian blood, as well as of Southern vivacity and quickness of temper.

During the next summer, Joan and Robert went home for Queen Victoria's first Jubilee. They stayed with Mrs Cantillon in London, and then went to Scotland as usual. The next year Andrew went to school in September, and two years later Antony, who, ever since he could lisp, declared his intention of being a sailor, went to a private school, where he was to be prepared for passing into the *Britannia*. It nearly broke Joan's heart to part with Antony. He filled the house with sunshine, and although he was perpetually up to mischief, and you never knew what he would be doing next, nor into what impossibly dangerous spot he had managed to get, he seemed to be watched over by some special Providence.

Andrew was a studious boy, who learnt Latin easily and was drawn towards serious things. Antony was bored with books, but he was quick at sums; he had a mathematically receptive memory and he liked buildings and pictures, but above all ships, and at Malta his passion was gratified. He had friends all over the Fleet. The year Joan and Robert took Antony to school, while they were still in England, Joan heard from Dr Valea for the last time. He was lying sick at Sorrento with a slight feverish attack but expected to be well again very soon. Up to that moment a fortnight had not gone by since he had left Malta without Joan having heard from him.

The next news she heard of him came a week later from his daughter, saying that he had suddenly taken a turn for the worse and had died three days after he was taken ill. A little later Joan received a pocket Dante in which he had inscribed her name and the date of the day he was taken ill. He had written at the beginning 'See *Paradiso*, Canto III', and there Joan found a line which he had underlined:

In la sua volontade è nostra pace.

Joan felt the loss as sharply as if she had seen him a few days before. The absence of his letters made an indescribable gap in her life. Her life within her life had vanished. 'My life,' she said to herself, 'in spite of appearances, is over.' But outwardly it went on exactly the same as it had done during the last six years. Joan had a husband whom she loved and respected, but with whom she could not exchange one intimate thought, and from whom she was separated by an invisible barrier of religion. To many people this would have made no difference. To Joan it made all the difference, and as the years went on she felt it more and more. Her boys were happy at school. She felt the absence of both of them; that of Antony acutely and every moment of the day. Little Kathleen, now seven years old, was becoming an interest to her, and was showing signs of marked character and originality, so much so that Joan felt as though she were a duck that had hatched a swan.

Robert lived an absolutely regular life. He saw as much as ever of Beryl Childs. He went out riding every day. Every now and then he pored over his collection of ivories, and sometimes he retired to what he called his work, namely, a translation of *Don Quixote* – he had now, after several years, reached Chapter 3. But Joan saw when they got back to Malta that winter that he had aged considerably, and she thought with a pang that were he to fall ill again in Malta there would be no Dr Valea to look after him. She had made friends with the younger doctor who had been Dr Valea's pupil.

Joan had innumerable acquaintances, and she saw Beryl Childs almost daily; but in spite of that she had no women friends. She was not a woman who made friends with women easily; nor did she feel the need. She had had one great outlet for intimacy in her life; and now that, with the death of Dr Valea, it was gone she felt she could never have and would never need another. Another year went by, and life seemed to have settled down in exactly the same rut. There was a new Governor; but the parties at Government House seemed to be exactly the same. There was a new C-in-C of the Mediterranean Fleet, the third Joan had known; but the parties on board the ships and the sailors seemed unchanged, although all the faces were different. The same play seemed to be going on; and although the cast was new the acting seemed to be exactly the same. And to Joan her life and Robert's seemed to follow the same routine: winter and spring in Malta; England towards the end of July; a few days in London and at Littlewood; two months in Scotland, as long as the boys' holidays lasted; then Malta once more. Only to Joan there was a great blank, and as the little steamer approached Malta in the dawn of an October morning the year after Antony had gone to school and Dr Valea had died, a year which stood out like a landmark in Joan's life, Joan said to herself, 'I am now middle-aged, and for a woman that means that life is over. Mine is empty anyhow, and there is nothing that can fill it again. My boys have been taken from me; that is just and proper. Kathleen is going to be completely independent, and is already a stranger. Robert can do and does without me, although he is unconscious of the fact. I am alone in the world, and I shall remain alone till I die.'

And as the steamer went through the gap in the high walls which lets shipping into the harbour of Valletta, the sun shone and struck the island, which seemed to blossom and change like the transformation scene of a pantomime. Buildings, sky and sea shone in a rosy and golden haze: a glory of hope and triumph. Whatever was to happen to Joan and her life, something had begun again on that October morning; and it was manifest that nature had no intention of retiring from business or shutting up the shutters of the many-coloured world.

CHAPTER 17

Joan and Robert had not been three days in Malta before they received an invitation to dine with the Governor, which they accepted. Joan was taken in to dinner by a Captain Luttrell, who was the Governor's new ADC. He had come out to Malta just after Joan and Robert had gone home. When Francis Luttrell had told Joan that he was to have the honour of taking her into dinner, beyond knowing that he was the ADC and a new ADC she had not seen before, she had no notion who he was; but his face, and still more his voice, stirred up sleeping memories in her mind, and when, as they sat down to dinner, he said to her, 'I think you know my brother,' she realized that this was Alexander's younger soldier brother from India whom she had never seen. She had never even heard much of him. She knew Alexander had a younger brother who was in India. Francis had been in India for the last six years, ever since he had left Sandhurst. He was just twenty-seven, ten years younger than Alexander. He was not very like Alexander, nor had he the good looks which had been distributed among the rest of his family;

but his irregular, rather monkeyish features were redeemed by laughing eyes and an engaging smile. His whole being oozed vivacity when he spoke to Joan about his brother; for the moment she lost her presence of mind. It was so unexpected; there was in Francis Luttrell's looks and voice something so like and yet so unlike his brother: and he had brought back the past with a rush to her.

'Oh yes,' she said, 'I haven't seen him for years.'

'He's an MP,' said Francis, 'Member for Southness in Easthamptonshire. He's been returned twice.'

'Is he a Liberal or a Conservative?' asked Joan.

'He was a Liberal and now he's a Liberal Unionist – in other words, a Conservative.'

'You think there's no difference between them?'

'I think there's no difference between any of them,' Francis said with a laugh, 'between Liberals, Radicals, Conservatives, Tory Democrats, or whatever they like to call themselves; I think the whole thing's a game, like cricket or tennis, and a very silly game too.'

'But they govern the country.'

'No. They make speeches and bamboozle the public; that's all they do. The country's governed by the permanent officials, and not badly either. But parliament's a farce.'

'Does your brother ever speak?'

'I think he has spoken once or twice. He's quite a good platform speaker. Quick at answering questions. Quick and plausible. The people like that.'

'And have you ever thought of standing for parliament?'

'Oh dear no,' he laughed, 'I hate politics.'

'I suppose most soldiers do. You like being in the Army?'

'I enjoyed India; but I had enough of it; and then I found soldiering in England absolutely soul-destroying. No, I can't say I like the Army in peacetime.'

'If you don't like the Army, why do you stay in it?'

'I'm afraid I'm not fit for anything else. I'm the dunce of the family.'

'I think real dunces don't know they're dunces. But if you are a dunce, I sympathize; I have been a dunce all my life. I was never educated.'

Their conversation was interrupted by Joan's other neighbour, a naval captain. She had felt the same ease in talking to Francis as she used to feel in talking to Alexander, but they had no more conversation that night till the end of dinner, when Joan said to him:

'Your brother didn't marry again?'

'Oh no, and he never will – now.'

'No?'

'It's too late.'

'Your eldest brother is married, isn't he?' said Joan, feeling she had better get off dangerous ground.

'Yes, and so is my youngest. He's a sailor, in China now.'

After dinner they played a round game. Joan said to herself as they drove home: 'He's easy to get on with, but not a patch on Alexander.'

'What do you think of the new ADC?' she said aloud to Robert.

'Not a bad chap. They say he's in love with the Governor's daughter. He was certainly very attentive to her tonight.'

'Yes, he was,' said Joan. The Governor's daughter, Alice Cobbe, had been sitting on Francis' other side. Nobody would have said she was exactly pretty; she was fair, with light grey eyes and a pretty skin; but a great many young and older men had already been in love with her, and she had had several offers of marriage. In spite of being neither pretty nor particularly clever, she seemed to attract everyone. She was gay and good-humoured, and she sang pretty sentimental songs, accompanying herself on the pianoforte. Robert was right in saying that Francis Luttrell was in love with Alice. He had fallen in love with her the first time he had met her at a race meeting in England, and that was the reason he had accepted the post of ADC

222

to General Sir Lawrence Cobbe, Governor of Malta; but ever since he had arrived at Malta he had felt that things were not going too well. Alice had so many admirers. She was charming to him; but she was charming to everyone else, young and old; to the Maltese nobility, to the admirals, to the midshipmen; to the colonels and the subalterns; the matter didn't seem to get any further. He saw Alice every day, and it seemed to him as if he never saw her at all; and if he sat next to her at one of her father's dinners, which he sometimes but rarely managed to arrange, she invariably contrived to rope her other neighbour into the conversation. That was precisely what happened at the dinner party at which Joan had just met him. He talked to Joan first, and then, when the opportunity came, he turned to Alice, but she roped into the conversation her other neighbour, the Colonel of the regiment quartered at Malta, and he – only too pleased to be so treated – never stopped talking to her, she casting a word to Francis every now and then, until dinner was nearly over, when he was obliged once more to talk to Joan.

That evening spurred his impatience to the verge of frenzy, and the next day, when Alice came to the room which was his office to arrange the seating of guests at luncheon, as soon as the business was at an end, he awkwardly and perhaps imprudently, with a great deal of stammering, hesitation and blushing, proposed to her. Alice did not seem surprised, and she quite simply and firmly refused him, saying she liked him very much but would never dream of marrying him. As a matter of fact he had taken Alice by surprise. She had somehow taken Francis as a matter of course. She liked him; but marriage – well, that was such a different thing, and then she dreamt of being so wildly in love with someone that there would be no question of hesitation or consideration: just one wild ecstatic affirmative. That, in spite of the proposals she had received, had never happened to her. Would it never happen? she wondered rather sadly. As for Francis, he was disconsolate. He had felt certain she would accept him some time, and now he felt he had come to Malta for nothing. He felt all at once solitary and friendless. The Army had bored him; Malta bored him still more. What should he do? What *could* he do? He was not exactly ambitious; that is to say, he had no wish to be an important personage, or to be either powerful or wealthy; but he felt he had something in him, and that there was something he could do and do well – if he only knew what it was – besides being an ADC, or soldiering in England. He needed confidence, or rather someone or something to give him confidence. He was to find this before long.

When Joan looked back on this part of her life in after-years she could never remember nor reconstruct how she had got to know Francis so well – so well so quickly. Of course Alexander had been the link, although Francis had no idea of that episode in Joan's and his brother's lives. Francis had made friends with Robert. They had ridden together and talked India for hours. Robert was constantly asking Francis to drop in. In about a month's time he was like one of the family; and Francis used to get the Governor to ask the Keiths to luncheon or dinner whenever he could. The Governor, a cultivated soldier, fond of flowers and music, liked Joan immensely; and his wife, who was silent and rather shy, but an admirable tennis player and proficient at every outdoor game and yet quiet and not horsy, liked Robert. His mono-syllabic conversation just suited her; she was in terror of what she called 'clever' people, and she felt happy and at her ease with Robert, while he admired her grey eyes, her neat figure and her hands well fitted for her admirable horsemanship. This did not make Joan jealous, but it made Beryl Childs jealous indeed.

Beryl Childs felt that a new twist had been given to the kaleidoscope of their intimate circle at Malta. She liked Francis Luttrell, and he liked her; but before long he began greatly to prefer the society of Joan. By

Christmas he had got to know Joan well; and he seemed to have recovered from the ill-success of his love affair. Beryl Childs and Joan discussed this one day together; they were sitting in Beryl's house.

'Do you think he is still in love with her?' asked Beryl.

'I think less,' said Joan. 'And Alice?'

'She told me herself,' said Beryl, 'that she could never think of marrying him.'

'Is there someone else?' asked Joan.

'I don't think so; but I think she is waiting for the impossible. She doesn't realize that men are all much alike.'

'I like her. She is a nice girl.'

'She would make a good wife.'

'I don't think she will ever marry anyone else.'

'Why not?'

'I think, although she may not like Captain Luttrell, she will never like anyone better.'

'And yet she can't find it too amusing at home.'

'When one goes there, Sir Lawrence is always in his study,' said Joan.

'Yes, a brown study. And then there's Lady Cobbe.'

'Robert thinks her charming.'

'So does Wilfrid. She listens to them and doesn't even interrupt. She just gives a faint inarticulate grunt every now and then which means, please go on. That's just what men like. They call that being easy to get on with.'

'Robert says she's such a good rider.'

'I believe she is.'

'She makes no fuss about it.'

'Oh no: she would never make a fuss. If she swam across the Channel she wouldn't say a word about it – I dare say she has. Nothing would frighten her. But what I think so odd is that she should have a daughter like Alice. Alice takes after her father. I believe he was gay when he was young. I think she's a fool, all the same, not to marry Francis Luttrell.'

'Perhaps she will,' said Joan.

Francis Luttrell did not repeat his proposal. He seemed, that spring, to be quite as happy as ever. Joan and Robert made plans as usual to go to England in July, in time for the boys' holidays. The boys came to Malta for Christmas but not for Easter. They spent their Easter holidays with the Baillies. Francis Luttrell announced his intention of getting some leave in August, and Robert invited him to stay at Killeen. He accepted readily. He arrived at Killeen for the 12th of August. The boys were there, and Kathleen and the Signorina. The Baillies were in Scotland too. Wilfrid and Beryl Childs were staying at their uncle's house, and Robert had been invited to go there when he liked. He chose the moment for going when Francis had been a week in the house. Mrs

Cantillon was expected, and Robert left Francis with Joan and the children and went to shoot at Laracor. Mrs Cantillon put off coming for two days, so Francis and Joan were left by themselves for forty-eight hours.

It was a hot summer and they spent hours in the garden. The time Francis liked best was the long twilight after dinner, when the sun's glow lingered in the west and the daylight lasted until eleven o'clock or later. The first evening like this they spent alone, when the children had gone to bed; they walked in the garden beside a burn which was banked on one side with herbaceous flowers – tiger lilies, phlox, monkshood and bergamots which were not yet all out.

Joan asked Francis about his future.

'I shall stay on at Malta for the present,' he said.

'And then?'

'Heaven knows. I can't go back to ordinary soldiering.'

'There are many things, aren't there, a soldier can do?' said Joan. 'There are places to go to, aren't there? Africa? Egypt? Besides which there nearly always seems to be a war going on somewhere. I suppose you will marry some day?'

'I don't think so. I haven't been lucky so far, but perhaps it's just as well. I expect you know all about my private affairs. I don't think I should have made Alice happy.'

'I think she is a charming girl.'

'She's wonderful. Nobody knows what she's like.'

'Have you known her long?'

'No, only a few months.'

'Well, you mustn't despair. I don't believe she'll marry quickly.'

'You don't think she loves anyone else?'

'I don't know. I know her so little, and that is a thing one can only guess when one knows somebody well.'

'Of course I had nothing to offer her.'

'Do you think she thought of that?'

'No, I don't think she did. At least I think she wouldn't have minded if she'd been fond of me. Only it would have made it easier for me if I had had something to offer; I mean some future. Prospects of some kind.'

'Haven't you got any prospects?'

'I should like to do something. I feel I could, but I don't know exactly what. I don't see what I can do if I stay in the Army; and if I leave it I don't see what I could do either. What I should really like to be would be something like a war correspondent. I like describing things – interesting things. That kind of thing.'

'Have you ever tried?'

'Yes, I have. I have tried to write things sometimes.'

'Can you show me anything you have written?'

'Would you really like to see it?'

'Yes.'

'Will you tell me honestly what you think of it?'

'I am very honest. I tell lies so badly. If I lied even a man would know it, stupid as they are.'

'You think men are very stupid.'

'Yes; very. Don't you?'

'Oh yes. I suppose so. Being a man, it's so difficult to judge. I have certainly never felt clever.'

'It's not that they aren't clever. Women aren't clever. It's that they are *so so* stupid. It's not necessary to be clever not to be as stupid as a man.'

'I'm sure you are right. Nobody could feel stupider than I do.'

'And yet for a man – you are not stupid at all. But even you are capable of being stupid. I expect you were stupid about Alice Cobbe.'

'I expect I was; but what ought I to have done?'

'I don't know; but I expect what you did was wrong.'

'Oh, it was. I proposed at the wrong moment; but I think it would have been just the same at any other moment.'

'You can try again.'

'Yes; I can try again. I wrote and told her that if she ever did change her mind now or later, or however long ahead, I would be there ready. I promised her I would never marry anyone else.'

Joan, thinking that this was perhaps the stupidest thing he could have done, said nothing.

'But it won't be any use,' he went on. 'Alice won't change her mind. Do you think, supposing I was capable of doing anything else, it would be silly to leave the Army?'

'No, I don't. I think it would be right to follow your vocation, if you have a vocation.'

'How can one tell?'

'It's difficult. I think it's a matter of instinct; one knows a real vocation when we come across one. I am sure my second son, Antony, will be a sailor. He has thought of nothing but ships and the sea ever since he could speak. I think he has inherited it from an uncle of Robert's who was an admiral. I am sure my eldest son, Andrew, will be something else: a scholar, possibly a priest.'

'It's easy to know about that kind of vocation, but in my case it's nothing definite; it's something vague. It is only that I feel I have no real vocation for the Army; and yet I like adventure. I want to do something, and I've a kind of feeling that I can describe certain things. At least they used to say I could at school, and I wrote some descriptions in India and sent them to newspapers and magazines and they were accepted.'

'That is what you are going to show me?'

'I have got some of them here; not all.'

Before Francis went to bed Joan reminded him that he had promised to show her what he had written. He went upstairs and fetched her an old number of the *Cornhill Magazine*. She took it to bed with her and read it before she went to sleep. It was the account of a tiger shoot in India She thought it wonderfully vivid and simple, and not, as she had expected, a bad imitation of that new and startling genius, Mr Rudyard Kipling.

CHAPTER 18

They had another whole day to themselves.
They went out fishing with the children and
had a picnic tea, baking potatoes and frying
the fish they caught. In the evening after
dinner they had another long talk. Joan told
Francis what she thought about his article,
and he was as surprised as he was delighted.
They talked more about Alice Cobbe, and
after Francis had told her in deep detail the
whole story of his love and courtship, Joan
was not certain that Alice was as indifferent
to him as he thought she was. She would
have liked to have heard Alice's side of the
story, and she felt sure that Francis had been
clumsy and had mismanaged the affair.

'She is sure,' she thought to herself, 'to
marry him in the long run – unless, of
course, there is someone else; and that we
don't know.'

Mrs Cantillon arrived the next morning;
and by the time she arrived Joan was aware
that she had crossed with Francis a rubicon
of intimacy that could never be recrossed.
Nor did the arrival of her aunt act as a break,
or check the rapid course of their acquaintance. It had become intimacy in an evening;

233

and it continued to be so in an ever-increasing crescendo. Mrs Cantillon noted this at once.

'I like Francis Luttrell,' she said to Joan. 'He's agreeable, but he's not got so much in him as Alexander. Not so much grit.'

'You think not?' said Joan.

'Alexander is far more solid and has better brains.'

'Perhaps, but I think Francis has more *talent*.'

'Oh! talent, what for? Does he paint or play?'

'No, I meant talent – for nothing in particular: just natural, useless cleverness. Alexander is more practical.'

'They say he's a good politician.'

'That's just what I mean. Francis could never be a politician.'

'It's a pity. I think he needs ballast.'

'He's still young. He may develop.'

'I dare say he will.'

'Have you seen Alexander lately?'

'He came to Littlewood for a night and I saw him in London, but he's too busy – too much occupied.'

'The House, I suppose.'

'Yes, and not only that,' Mrs Cantillon said with a sigh. 'There are other attractions – at least one.'

'The same one?' asked Joan, thinking of the American diplomat's wife.

'Yes; the same one. And Francis,' Mrs Cantillon asked, 'is he fancy-free? Aren't there any attractions at Malta?'

'He's in love with the Governor's daughter, but she has refused him.'

'Will she think better of it?'

'She may; but I don't know her well enough to tell. I know her so little.'

'For a heartbroken young man he seems to me quite gay.'

'He is *really* fond of her, I think, but I suppose nothing would stop a Luttrell being cheerful.'

'I think you succeed in keeping him cheerful, Joan dear.'

Joan blushed.

'Oh! I think he likes us. He gets on very well with Robert. Robert comes back to-morrow.'

Robert's return made no difference to the relations between Joan and Francis. Francis seemed to fit into their life easily and to become part of it. He stayed with them a fortnight. Then he had to go home before sailing for Malta. Joan and Robert went back early in October. They found Francis there, and life began again as usual; but there was one immense difference in it for Joan. She had someone now she could laugh with; and the official dinners and the round of gaieties, instead of being a burden, became a source of enjoyment because she had someone with whom she could share the fun; someone to compare notes with, talk things over with; someone who saw things from the same angle as she did; someone who talked her language. Not that she often saw him alone. She was fully occupied and saw a number of other people. The Governor entertained a great deal and had friends to stay with him, but Francis had no difficulty in arranging that the Keiths should be frequently invited to the Governor's luncheons and dinners; and he often managed to sit next to Joan. The months till Christmas seemed to Joan to rush by. At Christmas the Baillies came out to stay with her and brought the boys for their holidays. Andrew had left his preparatory school and was now at the Oratory. The winter season was more than usually gay, and Joan enjoyed it as never before. The summer seemed to her to have arrived so much sooner this year. She was longing to stay in Malta; but Robert wanted to go to England, and it was better for the boys to have their holidays in Scotland, and less expensive. Francis was not going home this year. The Governor wanted him. The Childs' went home in July; once more they were neighbours in Scotland, and once more Robert went to stay with them.

At the end of the holidays Joan and Robert went back to Malta, and soon after their arrival they were invited to luncheon by the

Governor. When Joan saw Francis she felt a pang of joy such as she had not felt for years; in fact she never remembered feeling anything quite like it before. Then she said to herself: 'Can I possibly be in love with him? It can't really be possible?' She was sitting next to Francis. There were many guests, and Joan was surprised not to see Alice. As soon as she got the opportunity she asked after her:

'She's gone,' he said gloomily.

'How do you mean gone?'

'She's got an aunt, Sir Lawrence's sister, who lives in Ireland, and she offered to take charge of Alice for a year. You know she's almost always lived abroad. Sir Lawrence has always been in foreign parts – India, Egypt, the Cape – so Alice jumped at the idea. She will love Ireland, and they will probably take her to London in the summer. They've got a daughter, just out.'

'But don't they miss her here?'

'HE does very much,' he said, lowering his voice. 'Lady C can get on without her. You know Alice never liked Malta.'

'You must miss her dreadfully,' said Joan.

'Yes,' he said. 'I miss her more than words can say. I haven't changed, and I shall never change, and she knows that.'

As he said those words Joan felt a wave of irrational, irresponsible hatred towards Alice, and she knew, once and for all, that she loved Francis. There was no disguising the fact. When he said those words he thought they were true; but, although Joan didn't realize it, they were no longer quite true. He had changed a little. That is to say, Joan was a factor in his life, and before he had known Joan there had been no factor but Alice. He had written to Joan often during her absence; he had confided to her all that was passing through his mind; and by so doing he had unknowingly created a tie and a bond which he was unconscious of. He was not to realize it for some time.

The Malta Autumn Season began, and Joan did not see Francis often, but whenever she saw him and for howsoever short a time, their intimacy seemed to increase in intensity and to be tightened.

Joan was like one in a dream. She did not probe the situation or question it. She did not face it. She floated upon it. When she was with Francis time had literally no meaning for her: she could have talked to him for ever. But she saw him seldom, and hardly ever alone. If they chanced to be thrown together and had the opportunity of talking uninterruptedly for more than two minutes, it was to Joan all the more precious from being so rare.

The brief snatched feasts seldom occurred; sometimes Francis called on her and found her, by the mercy of Providence, alone; and sometimes they were isolated, but not for long, in the Governor's garden at St Antonio; otherwise it was a case of catching stray moments on the wing. By Christmas Francis had fallen in love with Joan; but he was still unaware of what had happened to him, and then, in the month of January, Robert fell ill. The boys had not come out for Christmas this year; they had spent their holidays with the Baillies. Robert caught cold just after Christmas. The cold developed into double pneumonia; the attack was fierce and rapid; and after he had been laid up for a fortnight he rallied, and the doctor and the nurse said he was out of the wood. For two days he was on the mend. Then he had a relapse; and twenty-four hours later he received the last sacraments and died.

Joan decided to leave Malta for ever. She went home at the end of January. She saw Francis once before she went.

Robert's death changed her life. Although she had thought for the last three years it might happen any moment, and although nothing could have given her a clearer warning than the illness itself, when it did happen it came as a surprise, and the effect it had on her was a surprise also. She felt sadder than she had ever dreamt she could feel. It was as if the solid ground had been taken away from under her feet, and the world had been strangely and unaccountably darkened. In spite of this her feelings for Francis were unchanged. Although she had loved Robert and mourned him with all her heart, and with complete sincerity, this did not affect nor touch what she felt for Francis. They each understood the other in this matter, and neither of them said a word.

Joan said goodbye to Malta for ever. She went to England to her Aunt Amy. Francis continued to write to her regularly. He left Malta that summer, gave up the Army, and went out to Cairo, whence he sent the *Daily Rostrum* a series of letters, descriptive and political, which pleased the editor and the public so much that the newspaper took him on as their Near Eastern Correspondent.

Joan spent the whole of the next summer and winter in Scotland. The following spring she went to London, to Mrs Cantillon's. In London she met Alexander Luttrell. She was glad to see him again; but she had to confess sadly to herself that she liked Francis best.

In July Francis came to London from Cairo, and Joan got a letter from him on his arrival saying he must see her at once. She had never ceased hearing from him regularly, but there had been nothing in his recent letters which had hinted that anything of moment was happening to him. She told him when he would find her alone, and he came the next day.

'You know,' he said, 'the Cobbes have left Malta. They're in England now.'

'I didn't know,' said Joan.

'And Alice is living with her father and mother in the country – in Leicestershire.'

'Yes,' said Joan, wondering what was coming next.

'Well, I have had a long letter from Alice. It was waiting for me here at my club. She had sent it there to be forwarded, but I had cabled them when I started to keep my letters. I got it yesterday.'

'Yes.'

'Well, she says that if I haven't changed my mind she will marry me; but that if I have changed my mind she will quite understand.'

Joan felt a little bit dizzy.

'What will you say?' she said at last.

'That's just it. What shall I say? I suppose there is only one thing I can say.'

Then, as he said those words, Joan knew two things. That he *could* marry Alice Cobbe: that is to say, that he didn't love her as she loved him. She also knew she could prevent him marrying Alice Cobbe or, just at this moment, anyone else. She knew she had only to say a word, and she could do with him what she chose. It was as if she had met the devil face to face and he were offering her an easy bargain. She had only to exert her legitimate power, and take her due; angels would prevent her falling: it was their duty; there was authority from on high for it: and then she remembered a thing Dr Valea had said to her once. They were talking of *conflict*, and she had said that when it was a question of conflict between one person and another there sometimes came a moment when victory was in one's grasp but for a scruple, some scruple which warned one that the action was in some way selfish, unkind, cruel or illegitimate; but one knew if one took no heed of that scruple one could 'go in and win'; and was that perhaps not always the wisest course? Was it not foolish to heed the scruple? Perhaps the scruple was imaginary and baseless – an over-anxiety, a false claim? Were not the strong, the sane, the sensible, the right people those who went straight on, and were as incapable of apprehension with regard to the future as they were of regret for the past?

And Dr Valea had said to her:

'That is a difficult question, because although what theologians called 'scruples' are wholly blameworthy and ought not to be taken into consideration, to trample on a legitimate scruple, to be *unscrupulous*, is to put the soul in jeopardy. It is true it would give you the momentary victory, the fleeting triumph; but after it had happened, when- ever you went into a room everyone would be conscious you were a slightly less nice person.'

'I don't want Francis,' she said to herself, 'and the children to feel I am a slightly less nice person – shop-soiled.'

So Joan said to him:

'It is quite easy. You have only to be truthful. You want to marry her, don't you?'

'Yes – but–'

'Well, then, all you have to do is to tell her.'

Put like that it seemed so simple. Francis was in a sense relieved at having said what he had. He had feared at one moment he would not be able to. But at the same time he was bitterly disappointed. He had known what Joan would say, but he had secretly hoped against hope she would tell him his old promise didn't count. That is what he was expecting.

'You think she really likes me enough for me to marry her?'

'I am sure of it,' said Joan.

And as she said the words she felt the taste of a sharp and bitter disillusion.

'Alexander,' she thought to herself, 'would have behaved differently.' 'You must write to her,' she said, 'at *once*.'

CHAPTER 19

The next day it happened that Alexander came to see Joan at Mrs Cantillon's house in Hill Street. But Joan was out and he found Mrs Cantillon by herself. Mrs Cantillon knew that Alexander was at a loose end in life because Mrs Chalmers, the American lady who had played for some years the leading part in his life, had left England, her husband having been appointed to Berlin. Mrs Cantillon wanted Alexander to marry, and moreover she wanted him to marry one particular person.

She had often talked to him of marriage, and she did so again this afternoon.

'You really ought to marry again,' she said to him, 'and soon, or else it will be too late.'

'There's only one person I should care to marry in the world,' he said, 'and I am afraid she doesn't want to marry.'

'Who is that?' asked Mrs Cantillon.

'Joan Keith.'

Mrs Cantillon's heart leapt within her; but she was half afraid that Joan was no longer free. She had had for some time an inkling of the situation between her and Francis, but she did not know how far and in what

245

manner it had developed.

'You couldn't do better,' she said. 'Joan ought to marry again.'

'You think she will?'

'I'm sure she will; she's still young; only if you're not careful you'll be too late.'

'Do you mean,' he said, 'that there is someone else?'

'Oh no, but there is sure to be soon.'

'But she doesn't go out, and nobody ever sees her.'

'They will see her. As you know, Joan is very attractive and she is in great looks. Walter Bell met her here at tea the other day and he is going to paint her. He told me he thought she had the most striking face.'

'You're sure there's no one else?'

'Nobody that I know of.'

'I heard she had been quite broken by Keith's death.'

'So she was; but people get over those things when they are as young as Joan.'

'Well, I will try. When can I see her?'

'Come to luncheon tomorrow. You will find her. Walter Bell is coming.'

'He isn't in love with her?'

'Oh no. He only admires her as a painter.'

As Mrs Cantillon said this she looked at Alexander and thought what a fine couple Joan and he would make. Alexander looked young for his age; but time had mellowed without ageing him. 'He looks,' thought Mrs

Cantillon, 'like a Raeburn portrait – he has the right patine'; and there was so much fun lurking in his shrewd and sensible eyes.

That night Alexander dined out with a Cabinet Minister, and at this dinner were Wilfrid Childs and his wife. He had left Malta and had been given a Governorship, and was now on leave. Alexander sat next to Beryl Childs. He had never met her before and he was struck by her looks. They talked of Malta.

'Did you know the Keiths?' he asked.

'Oh yes. I knew them both extremely well. *She* was my greatest friend in Malta, I may say my only great friend; and he was such a dear. Wilfrid was devoted to him.'

Alexander suspected that there was something misleading in this version of the situation.

'There are children, aren't there?'

'Yes, three – two boys and a girl. The boys must be quite big by now. They're at school, and the girl, I think, will be pretty; she is dark, like an Italian.'

'Did he die suddenly?'

'He was only ill for a short time; but we all knew his lungs were bad and he couldn't spend the winter in England. He always had to be careful, and Joan used to look after him very well. Was the Captain Luttrell who was Sir Lawrence Cobbe's ADC any relation of yours?'

'He's my younger brother.'

'I thought you must be near relations; he is like you in a way. We knew him very well, and he knew Colonel Keith *very* well. Joan was devoted to him – you know her well, don't you?'

'I used to know her; but I haven't seen her for years.'

'Well, you know that she isn't a person who makes friends easily. She is difficult to please – fastidious and critical about people; but your brother got on with her at once; in fact she cured him.'

'What of?'

'She cured him of heartsickness. He was in love with Sir Lawrence's daughter, a most attractive girl. Everyone was in love with her, and your brother too, and we all thought she liked him, but when he did propose she refused him. I think if he had persisted she might have relented, but in the meantime he made the acquaintance of Joan Keith, and that cured him.'

Alexander felt a wave of violent jealousy surging up inside him.

'And did the girl marry anyone else?'

'No, not yet; she's in England now. The Cobbes have left Malta.'

Alexander changed the subject; he had heard enough.

After dinner he went straight home and wrote to Joan a passionate letter telling her that as she knew, as she must know, he had never loved anyone but her; that he had waited for her for years, and now the moment had come when he would and could wait no longer. He had been faithful to her all these long years. Everything had gone wrong, but now, at last, things had come right, unless they made another mistake. He was coming to luncheon tomorrow, and they would be able to talk afterwards.

By the same post Joan got a letter from Francis saying he felt he could not keep his promise to Alice Cobbe, and begging her to let him come and discuss the matter once more.

After breakfast, when sitting with her aunt in the dining-room, she said to her:

'Aunt Amy, Alexander wants to marry me. Would you mind if I did?'

'Mind, my dear child! it's my dearest, fondest wish.'

'You think it would be wise?'

'I'm sure of it.'

'You don't think I'm too old?'

'My dear child. You don't know your own power; you make other people look like paste, like imitation stones.'

'But, do you think Alexander would care for me?'

'He has always loved you. He loved you when he was engaged to Agatha.'

'Oh, Aunt Amy! how did you know?'

'I always knew. I saw it all; but there was nothing to be done. I suppose I oughtn't to have let you marry Glencairn.'

'It had to be.'

'Well, but now at last it will be all right.'

When Alexander came to luncheon that day he had no sooner looked at Joan than he guessed all would be well. Walter Bell, the painter, was there, and he arranged with Joan that she should sit for him.

After luncheon, when he had gone, Mrs Cantillon went out driving and left Joan and Alexander together. He then repeated what he had said in his letter.

'It isn't too late, is it, Joan?' he said.

'I don't think so.'

'There isn't anyone else?'

'No, not now. There was,' she said. 'Till yesterday,' she thought.

'Then at last it will be all right.'

'You must give me time to think it over.'

'I won't give you a minute,' he said, and he didn't...

She wrote that evening to Francis and told him that she and Alexander were engaged. She told him that she was sure that if he married Alice he would be happy. Francis was utterly astounded when he got Joan's letter. He could not believe it was true. He rushed round to Hill Street; but Joan was out. He scribbled a note, which he left for her, saying he must see her at once.

Joan arranged to be alone at five that afternoon, and Francis came.

'It isn't true, is it, Joan? It can't be,' were the first words he said, as soon as the servant who had brought in the tea went out of the room.

'Yes, Francis,' she said, 'it's true.'

'Alexander?'

'It's an old story. I knew Alexander before I married my first husband. I was in love with him. He was in love with me. He wanted to marry me; but I didn't know it. You didn't know?'

'I hadn't the slightest idea,' said Francis.

'Then things went wrong. There were misunderstandings; one big misunderstanding. It's too long to tell you in detail now, but it was cleared up too late, after Alexander had proposed to Agatha, and I was engaged to Glencairn. We had to go through with it, and I loved Alexander the whole time. And, what's more, if he had been free to marry me when Glencairn died, and if he had asked me to then, I should have said 'Yes'; I still loved him.'

'But do you love him now?'

'Yes,' said Joan, 'I love him now.'

'Oh, Joan, I don't believe it. I can't believe it. You can't do such a thing. You can't. I won't let you.'

'You will be happy married to Alice.'

'I won't. I can't.'

'You didn't feel like that yesterday.'

'I was mad yesterday; I am sane today.'

'No; it is the other way round. You were sane yesterday; you are mad today.'

'But don't you understand, Joan, that I hadn't realized till today what it all really meant. Don't you understand that I love you, Joan, and that I can't give you up?'

'I think you are really deceiving yourself. Try and realize that it is all out of the question, and you know really in your heart of hearts you've never loved anybody but Alice.'

'Till I met you.'

'And now you will marry her,' Joan went on, not taking any notice of his interruption, 'and be perfectly happy.'

'Joan, do you mean it?'

'Yes, I mean it.'

'You are really going to marry Alexander?'

'Yes, and he is coming here at six.'

This prosaic fact had more effect on Francis than any amount of explanation. There was something final about it. Francis looked at Joan and he understood there was no more to be said.

'Oh, Joan, I thought it'd all be different.'

'Things never turn out as one thinks,' she said sadly. 'Here is Aunt Amy.'

Joan had told her aunt that Francis was coming, and Mrs Cantillon had not needed a hint to know that Joan wouldn't mind if she were to interrupt the *tête-à-tête*.

'I must go,' Francis said. 'Joan,' he said to Mrs Cantillon, 'has just been telling me the news, and I have been congratulating her.'

'Yes,' said Mrs Cantillon. 'I am so happy about it.'

Francis went away; he wrote to her once more, a long letter of entreaty and expostulation, but he knew it was useless. The situation was settled.

He and Alice were married at the end of the summer, and directly afterwards they went to Constantinople. The *Daily Rostrum* wanted news from the Near East; the Sultan was said to be troublesome, and the period of Armenian massacres was about to begin. So Alice Cobbe was not yet destined to escape from the East.

Joan and Alexander were married quietly in the country, and they went first to Brockley, Joan's house in Suffolk, which no longer had a tenant. Joan did not re-let it, but Killeen was sold, and in the winter they took a small house in London.

And here this record of the story of Joan and Alexander Luttrell comes to an end; but their lives went on, and years afterwards their neighbours in Norfolk called them Darby and Joan.

In the summer of 1930, Susan Ray, Joan's married granddaughter, Kathleen's daughter, was staying at Brockley with her grandmother.

One night after dinner Susan was looking at an old scrapbook of Joan's that was full of photographs of friends and celebrities, statesmen, singers, actors, etc. She stopped at the photograph of Dorzan and said:

'Who is that, Granny?'

'That was a famous actress called Dorzan.'

'She's very ugly,' said Susan.

'We usedn't to think so,' said Joan, 'and she acted so well that it didn't matter whether she was ugly or not.'

'Did people really dress like that?'

'Yes.'

'It must have been a long time ago.'

'Yes,' said Joan, 'it was; a very long time ago.'

Presently Susan came to the photograph of Walter Bell's portrait of Joan, which was painted soon after she married Alexander Luttrell. The picture was thought to be one of the best pictures he ever did.

He painted her sitting on a chair, looking down, and dressed in black with white frills at her neck and cuffs.

'That's you, Granny, isn't it?' said Susan.

'Yes. It's Walter Bell's picture. It's in the Glasgow Gallery.'

'How calm you look!' said Susan. 'The Victorians always look calm. I suppose it's because nothing ever happened to you.'

'Nothing,' said Joan.